My heart was closed. Cold.
I was self-conscious and cynical.

These are the pieces of my un[...]
the small secrets [...] ectations
that defined [...]

But through this [...]iting,
I discovered a [...] the small windowless one
I had built for [...]
A world of softspoken beauty.

So here I am,
choosing to kick away the ladder
So that I may remain at your side.

I understand your solitude.
I see your shadow.

Tablo

2009. Feb.

Pieces *of* You

TABLO

Pieces of You

당신의 조각들

Mom and Dad.

Damon and Duke, I'll see you in heaven.

Andante   _8

Counting Pulses   _40

Breck   _84

The Rat   _88

Matchbox   _134

A Glass of Victory _144

The Walls of Our World _162

Hate Crime _168

Coup de Grace _186

Strawberry Fields Forever _224

A_ndante

I always make sure there's an opening in the room—an inch at the door, or maybe even at the window. My grandmother taught me that if one dies during sleep, the soul needs an exit, or it will be forever trapped in the room.

Two years ago, lying in bed, I heard a voice outside my door. It was silent enough to ignore; yet once heard, it burrowed in my thoughts. What I could no longer hear with my ears I did with my mind, and this was enough to keep me sleepless until sunrise.

Eventually, I was forced to close my door.

· · · · ·

It rained all Friday. The drive home was an ordeal through too much water in a city with too much attitude. My bumper would need a little work, maybe fifty dollars. My ears had taken the heavier damage.

By the time I got home, the rain had subsided into a light drizzle. After dumping my clothes in the dryer, I reclined in bed, drinking a glass of water while flipping through an ostentatiously large art book. Bruegel. Landscape with the Fall of Icarus. I took a final sip, put the half-empty glass on the bedside table, then closed my eyes.

The window was left open a little, not simply for me to

hear the rain, but for me to feel the city's light breeze. I lay there for over an hour, eyes closed but awake, imagining tiny raindrops exploding on my forehead. Soon my thoughts began sinking, slow like a feather falling, dissembling an overdue peace.

Then the voice returned. I could hear it through the shut door, even against the rain. For a moment, I thought I was imagining it. I wished I was.

I slowly rose to my feet and lifted up a curtain. Raindrops gathered like small spiders against the window's surface. They crawled slowly down the slick surface, touched the sill, and disappeared. Tomorrow would be another damp morning. I turned, flicked on the halogen on my desk, and put on my slippers. The lamp spotlighted a tiny picture frame. My father in a tuxedo, my mother smiling, both wrapped in a black and white youth now alien to me.

At first, I thought the voice was coming from the atrium. I stepped out, closing the door silently behind me. All the shoes were there. Even my father's heavy rain boots. They were dry. The voice was coming from the livingroom, a few paces down the hallway. It sounded like my father. I found myself wanting to ignore it, to walk back into my room and listen to the rain. But I walked on.

The hallway was my mother's pride. She affectionately called it *The Mishima Hall of Fame,* a shrine to her husband and son's excellence. I had always thought it was pretentious—framed photos, plaques, newspaper clippings covering both walls. When I had friends over, I would be a little embarrassed walking through it with them. Since my senior year in high school, however, I grew busy, and rarely had to worry about guests. The light seldom came on in the hallway since.

My father was sitting, alone, on the couch in the livingroom. He was a marble statue in the dark—a black, motionless shape silhouetted by the night's dim glow. I stood out of sight, standing halfway in the hallway, watching without listening. At first I thought the TV was talking—a baseball highlight was on the screen—but it was on mute. My father raised a hand, gesturing into empty space. A soliloquy in some forgotten play. I stood there for over an hour, never speaking, simply watching him speak to himself. I didn't know what he was saying. I didn't want to.

· · · · ·

I remember the most beautiful piano I ever saw. We had one in the house, of course, but it was nothing like the white Steinway at the Tokyo Bunka Kaikan Concert Hall. It stood like a grand swan—the hood raised like a magnificent wing, slender legs gracefully supporting its snow-white frame.

I was only nine then, too young to fully understand Mozart, but I watched in awe as the pianist swayed with each note. What I remember most, though, was not what I saw on stage. I remember the tiny Japanese woman seated four seats next to me. She leaned forward, possibly because she was hunchbacked, or maybe just to get a better view of the piano. She wore a sky blue kimono—an ocean of silk youth on an antique Japanese doll. At the first note, I saw her leathered face brighten, her almond eyes close, and her smile fold small flaps in her cheeks. She never opened her eyes again. Not even to applaud, not even to leave.

I remember being proud of my father in his elegant black tux, bowing to a standing ovation. My mother, teary-eyed, raised me on her shoulders. My father smiled—maybe for me, maybe for my mother, or maybe for the silent doll in the blue kimono. I remember thinking, for the first time, that I understood what greatness was.

· · · · ·

I woke up on Saturday morning, not in my bed, but in the hallway. I had fallen asleep while watching my father. I was immediately embarrassed, wondering whether or not he had seen me sprawled on the wooden floor. I felt strangely guilty. I rose and scanned the livingroom—the TV was still on, but the couch was empty. Outside, it was still raining.

"Did you stay up watching TV again?" my mother asked, emerging from her room. Her morning eyes were always dull—age had consumed her considerably in the last few years. I hesitated, glancing at the couch again. I nodded.

"Well it's the weekend, so I guess it's okay." She forced a smile and turned towards the kitchen.

"Where's Dad?" I asked.

She turned, eyes falling without meeting mine. I looked at the silver ring on my index finger; she looked at the clock above the couch. I could see a blurred reflection; she couldn't see much without her glasses. We were locked in a discordantly linked emotion, unable to be the first to react. She looked up. Walking. He was out walking.

I closed my eyes as my mother walked away.

· · · · ·

My father used to tell me that I learned to walk with my ears. One night, he placed his infant son on top of a piano, applying sound against his delicate skin. Soon, the baby's tiny feet were pacing around the black surface. I learned to walk to my father's andante.

On my eighteenth birthday, he asked if I wanted to go for a walk. For some reason, I said no. His face turned blank, and I wondered if he had heard me. No, I repeated. He nodded. But as I turned away, he asked again, do you want to go for a walk, Jonathan? I didn't know what to say, so without turning, I walked away. Sometimes I wonder if he knew what that meant.

. . . . .

I spent the afternoon helping my mother with her groceries. Saturday dinner was the only time the three of us would sit together in one room. I was at school during the week, and though I would only drive home from Julliard on the weekends, it was already enough trouble. At times when I wasn't busy, I lied. Until two months ago, Sunday had been another special day—we would attend church together. But my mother and I decided that it was too much of a hassle, and besides, my father didn't seem to believe in God anymore. So we had Saturday. An hour of Saturday.

Mom was a great cook, not only because of the meal itself, but because of the care she put into it. Three years ago, when I was sixteen, I was suspended from school for smoking in the bathroom. I thought I would starve that night, but she brought a small meal to my room. It was salmon. *Smoked* salmon, she said. She looked so beautiful that night. Forty-one years was a lie on this tall woman's flawless figure, on her wrinkled yet vibrant visage.

I remember hearing my father play Tchaikovsky a few days later. It was the last time anyone touched the Steinway in our piano room.

The food got worse over the years, but soon, I didn't even care what we were having. At times, it seemed like my mother would cook just to cook; I would eat just to eat; and we would be there, just to be there.

The grocery became my own *Hall of Fame* in a way. In every aisle, every rack, I would see my past in small boxes, cans, and bottles. Noodles reminded me of my father's sudden discomfort with chopsticks; pork, my mother being sick for days because of indigestion; and coffee, the nights when my father would sit with me, playing the piano and sipping only after each piece. My memories were canned goods; their only refuge, a small grocery.

Bach was playing as we picked out toilet paper.

* * * * *

Two weeks ago at Julliard. I played for four hours straight, never once stopping, not even for a drink of water. It was just me and the Samick in practice room B; me bitching with my fingers, and it listening to my every bitter word with patience. After any phone conversation with my parents, I would be there, in room B, playing until my fingertips bruised.

The world needs more crazy pianists, my instructor said, walking in on me one day. I hid my fingers, but the pain lingered with the last chord. Professor Meszaros smiled, sitting next to me. He was my mentor, yet I felt a strange unease in his presence. It could have been his inconquerable enthusiasm, or maybe even his heavy Hungarian accent. Five years ago, long before I had even considered Julliard, he played the harpsichord at the New England Conservatory of Music. My father performed with him once, years ago.

"Play something for me······ but ease up on the anger," he said. He moved off to the side, giving me command over the keys.

I began playing Beethoven's Piano Sonata No. 8. My bruised fingertips swallowed pain as they glided over the keys.

The professor whispered, you have your father's fingers.

I closed my eyes, and relished the pain.

· · · · ·

Driving back from the supermarket, I noticed my mother sneaking brief glances at me. I wanted to say something, but I kept my gaze out the window so that I wouldn't catch her.

My father wasn't home when we returned. I could sense worry on my mother's sullen face, but I comforted her only with silence. While she cooked, I sat at the dinner table, watching her move from one counter to another. I liked watching her work in the kitchen. Her eyes filled back with some forgotten life, her hands with industry that was now rare. In my memory, her hands were always white and their brilliance was magnified with the beautiful work they did. We used to fold origami cranes together, and I remember thinking that her hands were whiter than the tiny white sheets of paper we used. But age had given birth to sickly veins, and the less she used her hands, the more ugly they became. Even the last crane we made, flattened between the pages of some book in a shelf somewhere, must have yellowed with age.

．　．　．　．　．

I knew that my mother secretly wanted me to help, but I just sat at the table for over an hour, watching her work, watching the way she used to be. Where my eyes failed my imagination filled.

I helped her set the table once the cooking was done. Shark meat, scallops, wine. We were ready a little earlier than expected; the two of us sat at the table, dinner steaming, waiting silently. Occasionally, my mother's eyes would fall on the empty seat, and when I wasn't looking at her, mine would too.

"I'm thinking about taking a year off," I said. I hadn't really planned on it, but it was just something to say.

She nodded.

"Maybe I'll go back to Japan for a year⋯⋯ My Japanese

is totally falling apart these days," I continued. She nodded again, but I could see that she wasn't content. "If money's a problem, I mean with the treatment bills and everything, I could just stay with a friend and get a job. Maybe I just need some time away from music. Who knows, mom, maybe I'll find something new."

She didn't answer. I found myself wishing that my father would never return.

·　·　·　·　·

The doorbell rang, just once, and I knew it was him. I passed through the hallway and opened the door. My father stood hunched, soaked in rain. He had brought half the weather back with him.

Dinner time, he said. He crouched over to take off his

rain boots. But he just fumbled with it. I thought about helping him, but decided that it would be best to just let him try.

"Where'd you go?" I asked.

He didn't answer, continuing to fumble with his boot. The rain had uncurled his long, silver hair. He was still a very handsome man. He looked like an actor from some French New Wave film—sleek black raincoat, the nonchalance of an artist. But when he fell at the doorstep, tackling his feet, his momentous beauty disappeared forever. He was a helpless child that couldn't untie his shoelaces.

"Here, I'll help," I said, stealing the boot from his thin, aged fingers. It came off with a simple tug. He laughed. I suddenly wanted to laugh, to laugh with him, to sit there, or maybe outside in the rain, and just laugh with him. But I couldn't. I couldn't even smile. I just stood up and asked again, "Where'd you go?"

He rose slowly, placing a hand against my shoulder to support himself. Dinner time, he said.

. . . . .

When my father finished his meal, he poured himself a glass of whiskey. I looked at my mother, who had eaten almost nothing. Her gaze was dancing somewhere away from us. Somewhere more beautiful, I hoped. Her hair had grayed considerably. The two of them had misplaced their youth, and both were now too tired to look for it again. I watched my father down his drink with one big gulp. Minutes passed on the clock; years passed between the three of us.

That was the best salmon, he said. My mother smiled. I wanted to tell him that it was shark, but he would just be confused again. My mother asked if he wanted more and he didn't answer.

"That was *smoked* salmon, Dad," I said. "Remember when mom made me that smoked salmon?"

In the corner of my eye, I saw my mother frown.

My father poured himself another glass of whiskey. He silently toasted the air and threw it down. The ice clanked against the crystal glass.

It was painful to sit and watch him drink glass after glass, so I closed my mind's door on him, just as I would always close the door in my room to numb out his voice. When I did this, he had as much life as the bowl of fruit on the table.

"Dad, I'm going to Japan," I said, looking at my mother rather than at him. "Maybe I'll meet Mr. Saro⋯⋯ Remember him? Mom, you remember him, right?"

She looked away. I was talking to myself.

"Mr. Saro really liked our Steinway, remember? This one time, when Dad was playing at the governor's banquet, he joked about stealing it. He said maybe the piano is what makes the man."

No one was listening, so I played my own audience, laughing to myself. This must be how my father feels, I thought.

I looked across at my father whose eyes were wandering without moving. My mother's face turned towards me.

"Maybe I'll take the piano with me," I said to her. "I can just give it to him as a gift—."

Stop it, my mother said with her eyes. My father wasn't listening anyway.

"Let's just sell it, mom. There's no use keeping it here. No one plays it anymore. Why hold on to something when its owner has obviously already let it go?"

I stopped. I looked at my father, who had finished half the bottle. I knew that in a few more minutes, I could leave the table, leave this house, and never come back.

My father tapped his fingers against the table, delicately at first, then progressively harder.

．　．　．　．　．

Two years ago, a year before I entered Julliard, the Lille family prepared a banquet and recital for a few music scholars visiting from West London. Many from the classical community of New York and Boston attended. It was a full house, and my father was the main attraction.

He hadn't played for over two months, for personal reasons unknown to me at the time, and certainly to everyone else in the music community. I was sixteen and he was fifty-one.

He played a piece he had written in his thirties. A beautiful piano sonata entitled *Hana-bi*. He had performed it on a few prior occasions—the first time in Germany, then one time each in Paris and Japan. This was its debut in the States.

When he walked on stage, people applauded modestly, though their eyes screamed with admiration. My father sat at the piano, his hair neatly combed back, age exuding wisdom on every wrinkle.

But watching him, hearing his music spark gasps of admiration, a subtle melancholy touched me. All I knew of my father was what I had seen of him on stage or in the presence of a piano. Looking around, I saw that I shared him with a world of others. I didn't see anything that they didn't see, or hear anything that they didn't hear. I felt a sting in my chest. It was my first encounter with heartbreak.

That was my father's last public appearance. He stopped in the middle of his piece, unable to continue.

．　．　．　．　．

After finishing the bottle of whiskey, he left the table and walked out into the livingroom. My mother looked at me with disappointed eyes. I could see another wrinkle slithering under her eye, another black hair sickening to gray. I had to walk away.

My father was sitting on the couch. I waved my hand, gesturing without purpose. I moved closer and waved my hand again. His eyes were looking beyond me. A sudden sore stabbed my fingertips, and I turned away, my back against him. I wondered if he was reacting now, just when I could no longer see him.

I thought about leaving the apartment. I would drive back to school, maybe spend the rest of the weekend in practice rooms. Or maybe I would drive to Tisch and smoke up with a few friends.

I returned to my room and sat on the floor, looking up through the window. The rain had nearly stopped. The drive back wouldn't be all that bad. I closed my eyes, and in the darkness I could see my father's fingers glow.

* * * * *

An hour later, I found myself in a familiar yet forgotten place.

The piano looked like a grand corpse, lying under a sickly white sheet. I stripped the sheet away, slowly, making sure the dust wouldn't disperse. The black Steinway stood there beneath, as beautiful as ever. Its magnificence had been preserved through almost three years of negligence.

I suddenly remembered the white Steinway in Tokyo. This was our black swan, our ignored treasure.

The keys were brilliant white, as if untarnished by human touch. I skated a finger across the surface, feeling its smooth coldness.

It took me a few minutes to get used to the seat. I played a scale, almost inaudibly. Amazingly, the piano was still in tune. Sheet music was still resting on the holder, as if a ghost had been playing it all along.

I began Mozart's Sonata in D, Andante. The piano sang softly, filling the room, and the house, for the first time in years. But I was playing it wrong, furious forte, like a sprint rather than a walk. Each note smothered my mother's aging eyes, her graying hair, her strained brow. I wanted it to smother my father—the way he repeats sentences, the way he talks to himself at night, the way he sits staring at nothing.

· · · · ·

My mother was no longer in the kitchen when I came out of the piano room. She was probably in her bed. She heard me playing. My father did too, I suppose, but he was still sitting on the couch, his legs up on the coffee table. He was staring blankly at the dead TV.

"I played that at a recital once," I said.

His gaze roamed before settling on me. He said nothing. Just an empty stare.

"I played it better then."

* * * * *

The rain had stopped. I turned on to Spring Street, looking to bum a smoke. A girl I had dated back in high school was sitting at a curb with a couple of older guys. She didn't see me, and I was glad for that. She used to tell me that she loved the artist in me. I don't think she loved much else.

I decided to just buy a pack, so I walked a couple blocks to a bar and lounge on Thompson Street. After paying for a pack of Camels and a cup of coffee, I sat at the only empty outdoor table. Busy night.

Across the street was a Barnes and Nobles. I hadn't gone there in a while. There was one next to Julliard, but I stopped going once recital season started again. One week, I sat at the 'health & medicine' booth, reading every goddamn book on Alzheimer's.

I walked around Soho's streets for over an hour, running into familiar faces but never once stopping to chat. It was then that I felt something like a realization, something that was discomforting and comforting all at once. I didn't want to be here, in this city, anymore. And I no longer wanted to play the piano. Not even for a New York minute.

I wondered about a place without music—a place where my father would have been nothing more than a father.

· · · · ·

It was almost midnight when I returned home.

I thought I was at the wrong door. It was our building, 12th floor, but everything was startlingly different. I could hear a piano.

I rushed inside, and looked across the hallway towards

the piano room. It wasn't our Steinway. The music was coming from the livingroom. A strange déjà vu—just like the night before, I stood in the hallway, looking towards the livingroom with wondrous fear. I turned on the hallway light. Pictures. Black and whites. Blurred colors. Medals, plaques. The music grew louder with each step, and I shook with nervousness.

What I was hearing wasn't really a piano. It was just the stereo, playing an old recording. My father was sitting on the floor with his back against the couch. I looked around. My mother was probably sleeping now.

Not knowing whether or not he was awake, I walked to his side. There was a calm on his face, not the dumb calm of a sick man, but the cool serenity of an artist. He was awake, but his eyes were closed.

The recording was clearly made too close to the piano.

Some of the stronger notes were fuzzy. I sat next to him, careful not to startle him out of his peace. But he spoke before I could close my eyes.

"What do you hear?"

I didn't know if he was talking to me. He didn't open his eyes, didn't move his face at all. I stared in silence, not knowing what to do.

"What do you hear, Jonathan?" he repeated.

"It's Fur Elise, Dad," I replied. "Mom recorded you playing it on my thirteenth birthday." I was now breathing heavily, suddenly feeling claustrophobic. I wanted to stay, and at the same time, I wanted to disappear.

"What do you hear?" he repeated.

I wondered if he had heard me the first time. I kept my eyes closed. I felt his arm against mine, his soft breath beating slowly at my ear. The speakers exhaled note after note. I listened. I listened to my father's fingers dancing on the keys; I listened to my mother smiling beautifully in the afternoon light; I listened to me sitting in his warm lap.

"I hear the piano," I said.

"Jonathan, tell me what you hear."

"I hear you playing the piano, Dad."

At that moment, the piece ended. The last note lingering, the recording continuing in silence.

"What do you hear?"

I opened my eyes briefly to look at him. He wasn't hearing anything. He was trapped in a moment, a tiny gash in time.

"I hear you breathing," I said.

Counting Pulses

Winter, 2000

One

Mike held his cigarette out the window and pushed his face against the chill, humming a tune he had heard on the radio. He breathed in, letting a shot of the evening ride through his senses, mixing with the heavy and warm scent of the smoke. As he leaned his body further out, his gaze fell below the moon, careening down the lit and unlit windows of a nearby building till it halted at the street below. Cars moved fast, their tails of red and yellow headlights carving through the dark: parents heading home after work, kids shooting deeper into the city for a long evening to themselves. He picked out a particular car and trailed it with his eyes, traveling with it in his imagination till it disappeared at the distant end of his vision. He flicked the cigarette and let the evening catch it, swirling it into the dark nothing.

Returning to the kitchen counter, he poured the medication into a cup of water and placed it inside the microwave. After heating it for a minute, he carefully handled the hot cup with a towel and placed it on a plate on top of a small tray. He shut off the kitchen lights, and with one hand balancing the tray before him, stirred with the other hand as he walked towards his mother's bedroom. A thick thread of steam gently rose from the cup, fogging his glasses.

He nudged the door open with his shoulder, and, holding it ajar, looked into the small room and at the small bed where his mother had fallen asleep. The bedside lamp held a slow, dim light against a small black bible left open next to her pillow. She was snoring, and each snore ended in tiny, pitched breaths that sounded like musical notes. Mike stood at the door and listened for a brief moment, then walked in and put the tray beside her on the bed and gently tapped her awake.

"Oh my, I dozed right off," she said, shifting and smiling. A flush rose against her pale face, and Mike felt that she looked almost guilty about having fallen asleep.

"You must be tired," he said. "I was only gone for a few minutes." He closed the bible and placed it on the bedside table, next to her reading glasses.

"Don't read with this light."

"I wasn't really reading."

"Okay, but don't read with this light." He sat himself against the edge of the bed and stirred the medicine again. "Drink up."

She picked up the glass and held it to her lips, slowly sipping it. Mike watched her frail wrist and considered the slowness of the act, wondering if the cup was too hot or too heavy.

"You've been smoking again."

"Not really."

"Alright," she said, not looking up from her cup. "Are you going out?"

"I don't know. Drink that first."

She nodded and put her lips to the cup again. Mike watched the line of her neck and how each sip violently pulled on it. The whole thing was slow and burdensome.

"May sang at the assembly today," he said.

"She's a dear." She smiled and placed the empty cup back on the tray.

"I guess so. She was good." He picked up the tray and rose to return it to the kitchen. "You need to sleep now," he said.

She nodded and Mike turned out of the room, closing the door firmly behind him. He could hear her coughing, roughly and suddenly, as if she had been holding it in until he was gone. A long, broken sigh followed, and after listening to that, he walked away toward the kitchen.

By the time Mike finished washing the dishes from dinner, he felt drowsy and burdened, as if a heavy block was lodged in the back of his head and threatening to drop him head-first into the kitchen floor. He turned to the livingroom, where, he decided, he would fall asleep on the couch after a few minutes of television. He sat comfortably, placing a small cushion under his neck, and flipped through the channels and located the evening news. He lowered the volume to a droning lullaby and listened with his eyes closed. But he found himself actually interested in what the newscaster was saying—something about miracle healers in India—and after half an hour, he decided that the couch wouldn't work.

Originally, he had intended on going out with May, to see a late showing at the Film Forum. The two had been together almost the whole time after school, at a local diner, where Mike helped her with an essay she was writing for a scholarship to college. He was the only one who secretly knew that she wasn't all that intelligent, but her father was a very expensive clinical psychologist, and she was very good at talking about the human mind and convincing it to bend to her will. And she really did sing well at the assembly today. But he had to leave the diner to put his mother to sleep, and make her drink the medicine that she would surely forget to, and now he wasn't so hot about going out again. Besides, May wanted to see a French film and Mike was sure he hated French films, though he had never really seen one. And by now, he decided, she'd probably found some other guy to go with anyway.

Mike lay on the bed in his room, still wearing what he'd worn to school, and tried in earnest to sleep. He wished his stereo wasn't broken, since he always had trouble sleeping without music. According to May, because he had been overly "babied" as a child, his mother's lullabies had "conditioned" him. It annoyed him to hell when she talked like that, and he wished that he hadn't ever told her anything about his mother. He reminded himself not to tell her things in detail ever again, because at any given point, she would talk about them as if they were her own life experiences. He kept his eyes closed and hummed a tune to himself, deciding not to think of her at all, of who she was with now and why she hadn't called him about the movie.

He hummed song after song in the dark of his closed eyes, fatigue increasing painfully in his sockets. But he couldn't sleep, he just couldn't stop thinking about things, and he felt helplessly caught in his sheets, like a fish twisting and untwisting in the mesh of a net. Restless, he pulled himself out of bed and walked over to his desk, pulled a folder from his backpack and spread out before him pages of an assigned reading. With eyes half-closed and blurry, he read through the poem. When he got to the last line, he was surprised he had actually finished it but understood that he hadn't the faintest idea what he had just read. He looked over again at the blocks of words and tried to pick out the semblance of any meaning, but decided at last that it wasn't worth it. He was tired as hell, and nothing he could read would help his present condition. He thought about smoking another cigarette, but deciding that was too much work, he set his head against the desk and closed his eyes.

The phone rang in the livingroom, and Mike realized that he had briefly fallen asleep. With all his heart he cursed the loud ringing. He should have unplugged it since it would wake his mother, but he had forgotten.

He rushed to pick it up. It was Will.

"Bitch, it's freezing out here. Hurry up and come down."

"It's really late," Mike said, looking up at the livingroom clock and seeing that it really wasn't.

"The fuck it is. It's only eleven."

"My mom's sleeping."

"So come out."

Mike felt annoyed, but expected no less of Will's persistence. "You should have called before. You can't call here this late." There was a pause on the line and Mike hoped that Will understood.

"If you decide to come down, I'll be waiting in my car," Will said. He hung up and left Mike with a prolonged beep that sounded like a threat. It was always this way with Will. He made demands that resembled requests.

Mike put on his coat, walked over to his mother's room, and with great care, held the door ajar and peeped in at her figure lying still in the dark. Against the faint moonlight from the window, only a silhouette of her pale-toned pajamas and a few slivers of her hair could be seen. She wasn't snoring as before, and he feared that the phone call had awakened her. He softly stepped in and carefully crossed to her bed, whispering—*mom*—just audibly enough to ascertain that she was asleep. There was no response. He paused briefly, hovering over her, then walked to the far corner of the room, where he discreetly opened her purse and slipped out two ten dollar bills. He stuffed them roughly inside his pocket and walked out of the room, gently guiding the door closed.

He didn't really want to see Will, but he couldn't sleep anyway, and there really was not much else he could do.

Will wasn't in his car; he was standing at the main entrance of the apartment building, wearing a pair of shorts and sneakers without socks. He was smoking a cigarette, and with the other hand, dangling a small plastic bag.

"Too late my ass."

"You're a bastard," Mike snapped. "You could have

woken my mom up. What the hell you got in there?" He gestured at the plastic bag.

"Pipe and some good music." He smiled and took a long drag from his cigarette, fashioning himself as a gangster. "I got the goods, boss."

Mike watched the bag sway at Will's side and felt it suddenly drawing him, almost nauseatingly, to what was inside.

"Let's go," he said, turning towards Will's car.

"No, wait." Will held out a foot, stopping him. "Let's go up to your room."

"Are you kidding?"

"Come on. We'll be quiet."

"No, not tonight. How about in your car?"

"That's my mom's car."

"This is my mom's house."

Will shook his head disapprovingly.

"Don't be anal. She didn't wake up last time."

"Forget it then," Mike said. "You should have told me earlier anyway. I'm going out with May tonight." He hadn't intended on lying, but it sounded convenient.

"That's bullshit."

"What? I am."

Mike smiled slyly. "You're pathetic, man. I just fuckin' saw her going somewhere on my way here."

"She was probably heading over to the theater. I'm meeting her there."

"She was with another guy. You meeting him too?"

Mike paused uncomfortably.

"Stop being pathetic," Will said, taking a step towards the entrance of the apartment. "You coming?"

Mike cursed under his breath and followed.

Two

Mike told Will to go ahead to his room, then went to his mother's room to check on her. She was snoring again, in that pleasing, melodic way. He looked at her frail wrist and imagined that it must be cold to touch, and for a second, he thought about walking over and holding it between his fingers. He stood and listened to her snoring for a while, then, taking out the two bills from his pocket, walked over to her purse. The bills were slightly crumpled, so he pressed them straight in his palms before slipping them back in place. Leaving, he closed the door and pulled on the knob three times, listening intently to each firm click.

When he returned to his room, Will was sitting on his bed, playing with the buttons on the stereo on top of the headboard.

"What the fuck is wrong with this?"

"It's broken."

Will tapped his hand hard against one of the speakers and shook his head. "That sucks."

Mike grabbed a handful of clothes from his closet, and while Will packed the pipe, he placed them at the foot of the bedroom door, meticulously filling the gap between the door and the floor. Not even air, he hoped, could pass between his room and the rest of the world.

"See, we should do this somewhere else," he said, turning back and seeing that the pipe was ready in Will's palm. "We wouldn't need safety measures."

"Yeah, but it's cold outside and we would freeze to death. Remember winter break? That time we smoked out in front of Madison Square Garden? I got frostbite on my fuckin' balls that night."

Mike smiled hesitantly, then slowly broke into a laugh. Will smiled as the moodiness of the room eased up.

"They chapped. I had to use someone's lip balm during lunch time 'cause they hurt so bad."

They both laughed loudly this time.

The two of them passed around the pipe, inhaling and blowing out thick clouds of smoke. Mike held the smoke with seasoned precision, not letting any slip out through his lips. When it did, he stretched his neck and snapped his head, inhaling the smoke back from the air, like a fish breaking the surface of the water to suck oxygen. After finishing the round, they emptied the pipe, packed it, and passed it around again. They repeated this a few times, until both of them felt their heads deaden with weight.

"I," Will said, "am high."

"I, too, am high," Mike followed, speaking in a singsongy way.

Mike leaned his head against a pillow and closed his eyes, feeling his head sludge deep into it. His head fell far beyond the tangible surface of the pillow.

"I wish your stereo was working," Will said.

"Yeah, so do I."

"This isn't as good without music."

"Yeah, so do I."

Will giggled. "You just said that."

"Yeah, so do I."

"Hey, you're bugging out."

"No, you are," he said, looking up and staring at him as a doctor would a patient. "I'm just playing."

They laughed.

"It sucks that you're going off to college," Will said, suddenly not laughing anymore.

"Not really. I don't mind going somewhere else."

"You want to leave?"

"I want to see other places."

"Oh." Will said softly. "I can see what you mean, sort of. You gotta get up and go sometimes."

"That's right."

"I'm sorry. About coming over so late," Will said. He looked genuinely concerned, even though he was very high. "I know your mom hates me."

"That's not true. She doesn't even know who you are."

"I'm sorry."

"It's okay, but don't do it again."

Mike closed his eyes again and imagined what it might look like in California. He had never really left New York before.

Will nudged him and he opened his eyes.

"I need to ask you something."

"What?"

Will paused, falling silent, as if he himself had forgotten. "Never mind."

"No, tell me."

"I'll ask later."

"What is that?" Mike asked, leaning in abruptly. There was a fresh scar on the side of Will's head, just above the ear.

Will yanked himself away. "It's nothing." He turned so that Mike couldn't see the scar. "It's just a scratch."

There was an uncomfortable pause, and then they sat still for a while, silent in their respective, personal visions.

"May's one of those girls," Will said suddenly.

Mike had completely forgotten about her.

"I told you to watch out with her," he continued. "She'll

use you, and just at the moment you think she treats you special, you're reminded that she treats every other guy special."

"Yeah."

"You're not special."

"I know."

"What do you like about her?"

Mike considered it. "She's smart."

"No she's not."

"She knows all this stuff about how the brain works. Like this one time, she told me that people become conditioned to things if they get it a lot at a young age. You know what I'm talking about? Like music, you know, like music for me and how I'm always looking for it?"

"That's bullshit."

"No it's not. I'm so used to music around me that I can't

sleep without it now."

"Maybe that's true, but it's bullshit that you get used to everything, just because you get a lot of it. That girl's a bitch and she doesn't have a fucking clue on what she's talking about." He sounded strangely angry.

Mike rose from his bed and opened the window. The street below was nearly empty, with just a few cars heading home. A man and a woman were approaching the entrance of another apartment, with a small girl trailing at their feet. Leaning out, Mike tried to whistle a note into the air, but it fell weak in his throat and never made it out. He squinted his eyes and watched the rays of light from the streetlamps stretch out and touch each other, gathering into a halo and hovering over the street. It descended as a fluid floodlight, pouring over the dark asphalt paths and filling each crack and crevice. Everything and everyone below it— the large metal trash bins and parked cars, the man and the woman and their child—looked artificial in this bathing glow, and soon, the entire landscape looked staged, like a nocturnal theater coming to life only for those who watched intently.

He tried to picture May in his mind, wearing her customary brown turtleneck and plaid skirt, walking down some street in New York with a guy who could be anyone. Anyone at all, really, even him. He imagined leading her by the hand as if in a dance, passing stores along the street and swerving through the night without care. Mike wondered if May sang for this guy, or if this guy liked music at all.

"Listen," Will said, suddenly appearing at his shoulder. "I might need to sleep over here."

Mike took a moment to recollect his senses.

"My mom's not going to like it."

"Come on. I really need to stay."

Mike glimpsed again at the fresh scar above his ear, and, noticing, Will turned away.

"It was your Dad again, wasn't it?"

Will was silent. He rubbed along the scar with his finger and didn't say anything.

"You have to sleep on the floor, though," Mike said, cautiously.

Will returned to the bed to lie down, and Mike left briefly to fetch some potato chips from the kitchen. His hands were feeling clammy for some reason, so he opened the fridge and held them inside till they cooled. He thought about stopping by his mother's room again, but thought better of it and returned to his room quietly.

The two of them sat low to the floor against the side of the bed, crunching chips loudly. Mike was so hungry that he wasn't thinking about anything at all.

"What's up with your mom?" Will said, crunching.

"Don't ask that." Mike breathed slowly but with difficulty.

Will kept crunching and didn't ask again, and Mike wondered what he was thinking.

"She's sick," he said.

"With what?"

"Something bad."

"Oh." Will finished his mouthful and rolled the bag closed. "That sucks."

"It does."

The room fell silent, and Mike, for no reason, wished that he wasn't high anymore. He opened the bag and started crunching chips again, just so that there would be something to listen to.

Three

Mike had no idea what time it was, but judging by the glow that filled the room, giving just enough light to make everything look like a black and white film, the sun would rise in a couple hours. Then his mother would be up.

His head had been swirling fast in stuttered waves, a bit too fast, for over ten minutes now. He began to worry but decided not to say anything. He looked for diversions.

"You want to see something cool?" he said, rising off the floor and gesturing towards the door. His feet felt swollen, and as the two of them walked out towards the livingroom, Mike moved clumsily and dumbly across the cold floor.

"What if your mom wakes up?" Will asked.

"Don't worry about it."

Mike led him to an oak cabinet in the corner next to the

couch. Squatting, he opened it with a squeak and revealed a large heap of vinyls. He skated a finger across the tops of the plastic covers, tracing a clear line through the thin film of dust.

"That's cool," Will said with emotion. "Didn't know you had records."

"Check this out."

Mike pulled out one of the vinyls and handed it to Will, who stretched out his hands and let it rest gently on top of them. It was faded pink and wrapped in some sort of protective plastic that was tattered at the edges.

"Shit, that's your mom, isn't it?" Will said, leaning into the cover photo with surprise. "Melly Milne?"

"This is before she became Melissa Platt."

Will scanned the cover with genuine interest, running a finger along the rough edges.

"That's really cool. I didn't know your mom was a singer."

"She was."

"She had, like, records."

"Yeah, three of them." Mike felt pride slipping into his voice and it made him nervous, so he added, "But that was a long time ago."

"Can you play it?"

"We don't have a phonograph anymore."

"Then how do you listen to it?"

"We don't."

The swirling in Mike's head suddenly intensified, almost painfully coursing through to his eyes. His mouth felt too dry.

"I want some water," Mike said, taking the vinyl rudely back from Will. He placed it back inside the cabinet and headed towards the kitchen.

"You alright?" Will asked, following shortly behind him.

Mike poured himself a glass of tap water and drank it down quickly. He took a few long breaths and then had another glass. Then he felt better.

When they returned to his room, they cleaned up a little, and then Mike shut off the lights and they both tried to sleep. He gave Will a coat to use as a blanket on the floor. Then, lying on his bed, he put a hand against his chest and tried to feel his heartbeat. It was slightly fast. He closed his eyes and tried not to think about it.

"What's going to happen when you leave?" Will asked, after being silent for a long time. "I mean, if your mom is sick and all."

Mike didn't answer.

"Who's gonna take care of her?"

His heartbeat was picking up, thumping warm against his palm, and he strained to press harder against his chest.

"What's wrong with her, exactly? Is it like cancer or something?"

With sudden force, a thick, coarse stream of vomit shot up to Mike's throat and caught itself there, splitting his senses. He placed a hand on his chest and raised himself a little to face Will, half-visible in the growing light outside.

"Shut up."

Will looked back at him funny. "No, I'm being serious."

"The fuck do you care?"

"I'm just asking."

"Well, shut up now."

Mike turned away. He really wished the stereo was working, or for just any sound at all to fill the room and drown out the sound of his heartbeat. He wondered why he was so mad. He suddenly felt guilty and started sweating.

"I'm sorry," Will said.

Something burst inside Mike's chest, spilling pulses that shot up through his neck into the side of his head. He placed a hand against it and realized that he was sweating a bit too much.

"Will, check my pulse."

Will opened his eyes and slowly turned to him. "What?"

"Check my pulse, quick."

He stared dumbly for a moment, then seeing that Mike was shivering, he walked over and placed a finger against his neck and looked for a pulse.

"Got it," he said. Mike's neck felt very hot.

"I'm gonna count fifteen seconds. Tell me how many times it beats."

"Okay."

"One······ two······"

"Wait, you're counting too slow."

"Are you sure?"

"Yeah, that was like four seconds."

"Okay, you count fifteen then." Mike placed two fingers against his wrist and located the pulse. "Go."

"One······ two······ three······ four," he counted, careful to keep pace. "Fourteen······ fifteen······ stop. How many?"

"Are you sure that was the right speed?"

"Mike. I'm high too."

"Thirty-five. Thirty-five times four."

"What is that?"

"One hundred and eighty." Mike's face turned red and heated, and he was sweating profusely now.

Will quickly turned on the room lights and rushed over to his desk, finding a calculator. "Wait, what was it?"

"Thirty-five."

He punched in the numbers. "One hundred and forty."

"Shit."

"Is that normal? What's normal?"

"A hundred, I think."

"Fuck." Will rushed over and tried to force the blanket over him, but Mike pushed him away.

"No, no, open the window."

"I'm gonna call an ambulance."

"No."

"Yes."

"Don't fucking call. My mom's going to wake up."

"Do you have any idea how red you are? What if you die?"

"No one dies from smoking pot."

"True."

"I'm okay, just open the window."

"It's open."

"Check my pulse again."

Will checked and rechecked Mike's pulse, and each time, it increased. Mike began coughing and moaning painfully. He struggled to keep an eye open, feeling his eyelid throb in rhythmic beats, and saw that Will was sweating as well. Mike watched him pacing the room with hands deep inside his hair, shaking his head violently. Fear soaked into Mike's back.

"We need help," Will said, suddenly not moving.

Mike tried to speak, to tell him not to leave, but Will rushed out of sight before he could muster the strength.

His back flat against the bed, Mike gripped the sheets beneath him with intense pressure, fingernails shooting into his palms. The texture was slipping out of his hands, losing tangibility, and he felt as if he were trying to brace himself against the surface of a deep body of water. He closed his eyes and listened to the soft thumping in the side of his head.

He whispered—*Will*—but feared that he wasn't making any sound. He whispered again and again, louder, but there was no answer. A surge of fatigue and confusion pushed out a tear in one of his eyes. He wondered if Will had run home.

There was a loud crack—the metal knob hitting the wall—as the bedroom door opened, and Mike snapped his head up to see Will rushing in, breathing frantically. Mike's mother was moving slowly behind him, led by Will's shaking arm.

"I checked his pulse," Will said, speaking rapidly now. "It's really, really high. I was gonna call the ambulance but he wouldn't let me."

She looked over at the pipe on the floor, then at Mike. He wasn't sweating as bad anymore, but his breaths were still sharp and frightfully fast. Mike's mother pulled her hand away from Will and fell to her son's side on the bed. She pressed a palm against his chest and noted his heartbeats.

"You can go home now," she said, looking up at Will.

"I'm sorry, I'm really sorry."

"It's fine. Go home." Her voice trembled.

"Let him stay," Mike said from below her. "He can't go home."

Will stood murmuring more apologies, then dropped against the wall in the corner of the room. He took a few prolonged breaths, then closed his eyes.

Mike's mother placed a hand on her son's forehead, feeling the clammy heat. "Dear," she said. "I'm going to call the ambulance."

"I'm so sorry," Mike answered, struggling to open his eyes.

"You just stay put and try not to move, okay?"

After dialing for the paramedics, she returned to his side with a towel and a cup of hot water. She gently wiped across his arms and legs, drying the sweat away. Help was on its way, and all she could do now was keep him awake. "It's going to be alright," she said. She held the cup to his lips, carefully pouring all the water into his mouth. She then wiped his lips dry.

"I'm sorry," he whimpered.

"More water?"

"Mom, I'm sorry."

"It's alright. Do you want more water?"

"No," he said. He lifted a hand and rested it gently against her knee. "Sing me a song."

"A song?"

"Yeah." He coughed again.

She sat silent and immobile. She was confused.

"Sing me a song, Mom," he repeated. His chest rose sharply against her small hand.

She nodded hesitantly, then slowly, in a frail voice, eased into the first verse of *American Pie*. She closed her eyes and sang, realizing how weak her voice had become, and fearing that Mike would notice it. But she kept singing.

Bye, bye Miss American Pie
Drove my Chevy to the levy but the levy was dry
Them good ol' boys were drinkin' whiskey and rye
Singin,' this will be the day that I die

"Mom," he said, cutting into her voice.

Today is the day that I die

"Mom, stop," he repeated, gripping his hand tighter against her knee.

She opened her eyes and stared back in surprise. Then, realizing what she had just sung, she placed her hand over his and said, "Oh no, that's just what the song says."

"I know," Mike said. He felt a tear stream down his cheek.

"Don't worry." She leaned closer to his face and wiped his eye dry with a thumb. "Help is coming."

Mike suddenly felt embarrassed that he had asked her to sing. He giggled nervously. And Will, who had been dozing off, opened his eyes and giggled too. Mike gripped his mother's hand tightly and pulled her down beside him. "I'm going to be okay."

"Help is coming."

Mike looked past his mother at Will, sitting in a silent lump in the corner of the room.

"Will, I'm sorry," Mike said, in a damaged voice.

"Don't talk," Will said.

"I'm sorry about tonight," he continued, gasping lightly. "This must be the worst high you've ever had."

Will put his head in his hands, and Mike wondered if he had heard.

"If you get okay," Will said, looking up again, "this is gonna be the best high I've ever had."

"Help is on its way," his mother repeated.

Mike struggled to wrap an arm around her. It had been a long time since he had held her, and he realized he had grown considerably, because her body felt much smaller than he remembered. "Let's just sleep. Let's forget about it and just sleep."

A thought entered Mike's head. The thought that if one of these people ever needed a protector, or a saviour, he would try to be just that.

As sunrise slowly swelled against the window of the bedroom, Mike braced his mother precariously in his shaking arms, imagining that they would fall asleep just like this, the three of them together, never ever having to leave.

Break
Fall, 1998

Once the kids left the class, Frank sat on his hard steel chair for the first time and caught his breath. The dry, stale chalk on his hands felt odd, and he thought of moth balls, crushed and packed in his palms.

It was spring but now the blinds were shut, the lights were off, and a chill sat on his arms like thin dust on an aged book.

Not much time. The kids would be back soon, and with

them he would have to hold his breath for another hour.

It was a good thing, at times like this, that Frank kept the rum in his desk. Of course, no one knew. No one at school and no one at home. There was a small can of breath mints in the desk as well, so it was alright.

He took four quick sips of the rum and shut his eyes. He wished for the quiet of the room to take him by force, to blank out the math, the books and all the words of the past hour.

You need a break. Words of old friends, rich friends that should have died by now, whom he saw at a bar last night. *You should take a break, Frank. Travel.*

He hid the rum and dropped a few mints in his mouth and thought of where he would go, if he could go, if he could just get up and go.

But the bell, like a shot from a gun, brought the storm of voices back into the room and pierced his chest.

Break_87

The Rat
Summer, 2000

The rat lumbered through the open door into Mark's bedroom, stepping across a shirt, a pair of boxers, and finally setting itself atop a stack of papers. Its whiskers moved with the deep, defined rhythm of its underbelly, mechanical breaths that rumbled like an engine. The way it tilted its head up with the afternoon light from the window glazing its thick coat, almost made it appear intelligent, as if it was patiently awaiting the answer to a grave question.

Mark awoke and immediately felt around with his small hands, understanding that the girl was no longer there. It had become a morning routine to do so, an act as meaningless as the dream he was waking from. He paused, breathed a short sigh, then rolled over to bury his face against the pillow. He was surprised at the pleasant scent her hair had left lingering behind. He let himself fall into it, but soon the smell became unidentifiably monotonous, like a color laid over a similar color, until it was completely lost.

Slowly turning to face the room, he eased out of the sheets and dropped one leg to the floor. The rat's tail pressed coldly against the bottom of his foot, and Mark snapped it away, throwing his body back across the bed. A sharp spasm shot up to his thigh, and he slapped his palm against it, pinching gently with his fingers. Placing a hand against the wall for balance, he slowly stood up on the bed and retreated with his back curving against the low ceiling.

The rat calmly tilted its body and faced its tail. It was impossibly large: the top of its head would easily rise up to Mark's knee. Science fiction. Giant rats flooded the streets, buzzing like a bee-storm, pouring from outgrown tunnels and multiplying like cells. The rat faced him, arching its shoulders over its head, a menacing heap of black and brown rising in his direction. It turned its head up and puffed, blowing its whiskers gently. Mark leaned harder against the wall, bewildered. He searched the bedroom— unread magazines on the floor, loosely hung shirts inside his opened closet—and recognized that it was his own.

He carefully crouched and leaned to fetch his organizer and cellular phone from his desktop, watching the rat's head follow his movements. Its eyes looked disapproving. Retreating again, Mark scanned the room for other things he would need, only the bare necessities, then squatted on the bed, careful to keep a safe distance from the rat. He ripped out a page from his organizer, crunched it into a ball, and threw it to the opposite corner of his room. The rat turned but didn't follow.

Unable to think of anything else, he planted the organizer and his phone under his arm and leaped over the rat towards the door. He lost his landing and one knee slammed into the floor, sending a tremble straight up to his neck. He turned and faced the rat, now eye-level and crouching as if to leap. Breathless, he shuffled to stand, gripping his things tight against his chest. The rat took a step forward and Mark quickly turned out of the room, slamming the door behind him.

Mark dropped to the floor and gripped his knee with a hand. The rat was seemingly right up against his back, clawing and scraping the door. The moment was so eerily ridiculous that he wanted to laugh, but he had trouble catching his breath.

When Hamilton arrived, Mark felt that his world would slowly shape back into normalcy, which was what happened whenever Hamilton was around. He was wearing his trademark hat, black and brimmed, precisely arranged to lean towards one side of his head.

Mark offered him a cup of coffee, which was declined with a gesture, then pulled up a chair next to the couch and sat. He was aware of a sudden shake in his hand, and had to put his cup down to avoid Hamilton's disapproval.

"How's it going?"

"I'm a little shaken up, actually."

Hamilton looked confused. "No, I meant the girls."

Mark looked at the bruise on his knee and wondered how long it would last. He could still feel the rat's tail across the bottom of his foot, stamped like a scab. It didn't seem important where the rat came from, only how it had fit through any hole into the apartment. And where was this hole?

"Mark?"

He looked at Hamilton, who looked confused, or maybe just annoyed or impatient. He had lit himself a cigarette.

"What's with the knee?"

"Banged it against the door."

Hamilton laughed, too long, and the sound of it made what Mark said completely unimportant. He cleared his throat and continued, "The girls. Have you decided?"

Mark stared back as if they had just discussed this at great length. "It's either Amanda or Valerie."

"Oh not Valerie. No, not her. She's no good."

"Then it's Amanda."

"She's good?"

"She's decent. I was thinking her over Valerie anyway."

"And her figure?"

"The same as Valerie."

"Price?"

"A little lower."

Hamilton rubbed his chin. "Did you talk about the nudity?"

"Only what's in the script."

"You got any photograph?"

"No."

"Good. I'd like to be there for that."

"Sure."

Hamilton cleared his throat again, then nodded. "You see that Julius Caesar yet?"

Mark shook his head and looked back at the bruise. He placed a finger on it. The pain was grossly pleasurable.

"It's got a Black Antony. Wise casting, no doubt about that." He said it as if he himself had accomplished this. "Adds *color to* those bland columns, you know?" He took a puff from his cigarette and held it up, looking to Mark for an ashtray.

"Just put it out on the table."

Hamilton hesitated, then did as he was told, ashing on the table. He looked back at Mark. "You alright?"

The question was interrupted by a phone call, and Mark retreated into the kitchenette to answer it. It was vermin control.

"You left a message with us." The voice was gruff.

"I need an exterminator."

"You want to make an appointment?"

"No, I need one now."

"That's really not how this works." There was an uncomfortable pause. "Earliest we can do is tomorrow."

Mark felt something like a bite at his foot. He glanced over at Hamilton, who was now up and lumbering around the livingroom. "Do you know anyone else? A freelancer? I can't possibly wait till tomorrow."

"No. You won't find anyone that soon. What's the problem?"

Mark sighed. "There's a rat in my apartment. It's the size of a Chihuahua."

Hamilton looked up from a book he had found. The voice on the line chuckled, then there was silence, as if a hand was cupping the receiver. Mark could almost see this fat man on the phone, watching football or something, snickering as he told his buddies.

"I can send someone over tomorrow," the man said, returning on the line. "I don't do the actual runs, or I would go over there myself, just to see this thing."

Mark felt that it was the best he could do. "Alright."

Hamilton looked up from the couch as Mark returned to the livingroom. He had put out his cigarette on the coffee table and was now stretching his arms above his head.

"You got a *rat* in here?" He apprehensively scanned the floor, his hat slightly slouching over the side of his head. "How'd it get in here?"

"Through the door, I suppose."

Hamilton looked confused, observing Mark as one would a page of indecipherable jargon. He fixed his hat, then placed what he was reading on the coffee table, and Mark was surprised to see that it was his photography portfolio. He hadn't even remembered where it was.

"These are pretty good," Hamilton said, nodding to himself. "You should do something with these."

"Can you put that back?"

"No, I really like these. I had no idea." He turned through the pages, as if to show Mark something he himself had done. "I could set you up with something if you'd like."

"It's fine."

Mark watched Hamilton's hat bounce as he nodded and realized just how much he disliked the man. He was one of those directors that acted as if he had lived a thousand years and had stories to tell from every damn second of it.

"Casting suits me fine right now," Mark said. He closed the portfolio, picked it up and placed it under the coffee table.

Hamilton shrugged his shoulders and nodded again, uneasily. A strange awkwardness flooded the room, and it became apparent to both men that Hamilton had outstayed his welcome. Mark led him to the door.

"So where's this rat?"

"In the bedroom."

"It's confined then."

"I guess."

Hamilton smiled, both ends of his thick brows arching up. "Puts a damper on the casting though, huh? No casting bed." He laughed, and Mark stared back emptily. "Oh, you should see this." His hand dug into his pocket and came out with a small brochure. He handed it to Mark.

"What is this?"

"I told you about my kid? He just finished up at Tisch. His film—this one right here—it just got picked up."

Mark flipped open the brochure and read it: *Citizen Shame.*

"It's a documentary. On *Citizen Kane*."

Mark folded it into his pocket. "How clever."

"The kid's a wunderkind, no doubt about that. I actually discouraged him from film, you know, told him to try politics or something, something more secure I said, but these kids are really taking over now. We are dinosaurs."

Mark nodded as Hamilton explained the metaphor.

After he left, Mark returned to the livingroom and sat at the couch. He had planned on doing something before Hamilton arrived, but now had trouble remembering what. He finished his cup of coffee, put it down, and picked up the dead cigarette Hamilton had left lying on the table. He looked at it for a while, then put it between his lips and walked over to the kitchenette to find matches. The cabinet where he kept them was filled with junk—a half-eaten chocolate bar, used saran wrap, condoms—and he had to empty it out to find the matches. He left the junk on the kitchen top and walked back to the couch. The cigarette tasted horrid, and Mark hadn't smoked anything for a while, but he kept it at his mouth and picked up the portfolio under the coffee table.

He glanced at the first page: Mark Wallace, Advanced Cinematography, Tisch School of the Arts. The next page was a dark, heavily contrasted photo of a man sitting naked at a bus stop, with a frail, damaged hand feeding a blindingly white dove. Mark read the caption out loud: "Stripped bare, a man discovers Peace."

He rubbed a finger across the image, trying to remember what it was like, that second year in film school, waiting for the last bus back to campus and finding that man—that perfect shot. The image belonged to him, but staring at it now, he had trouble believing that he had any part in the creation.

He fixed an invisible hat on his head and said out loud, "This is *clever.* I had *no* idea!"

He closed the portfolio and leaned over to slip it under the couch. Then he snubbed out the cigarette on the table, making a companion mark next to the one Hamilton had left.

For a brief moment, he had completely forgotten about the rat.

The best way to tell Amanda Rich about the part, Mark decided, was to invite her over for dinner. It wasn't a necessary procedure, but he had always felt it customary. As a colleague once said, "Casting is like grocery shopping for someone else, like your mother. You buy the best ingredients, shit that'll knock the socks off your brothers and sisters, but she takes it, fucks it all up, and spits out some bland casserole". Mark took it to simply mean that an actress, once the production began, could no longer be his.

With the phone on his lap, he flipped through his organizer for Amanda's number but couldn't find it. He flipped through it again, scrutinizing every memo, then fearfully realized it was lying on the floor next to his bed. "Rat-litter now," he said to himself.

Approaching the door with caution, he put an ear to it to check for breathing. He could hear a muted rustling at a safe distance, so he opened the door just a little and peeped in through the gap. As he feared, the rat hadn't moved, and was still settled atop the pile of papers next to the bed. The resumes of the actresses. Amanda's number.

He closed the door and considered whether he was truly afraid of this rat. He had once watched his father in the kitchen with a frying pan, beating a rat to a pulp as his mother held him from a distance and screamed. "It's just a rat," his father said. Mark had a feeling, though, that even his father would have thought twice about this one.

But Amanda's number was in there, so was his entire evening, and he needed that desperately. He cursed to himself and screened various scenes in his head. He could just rush the damn thing, scaring it off under the bed. But he wondered if it would even fit under, and the whole thing sounded like the beginning of a story someone would tell in explaining how he had happened to get such a nasty scar on his face. It was all too risky.

He fetched a broom from the kitchenette and returned to the door, opening a small gap and eyeing the rat. It didn't seem to notice that he was watching. Holding the broom by its head, he pushed the stick carefully and silently till it was a few inches from the rat, then with sudden, violent force, shoved the end into its side. The rat, like a touch-sensitive toy, jumped and darted forward, disappearing under the bed. Mark rushed into the room, grabbed the stack of papers and fumbled to keep it in his hands as he ricocheted out, slamming the door behind him.

He felt a ridiculous sense of accomplishment as he returned to the livingroom and searched through the papers for Amanda. He skimmed through pages of faces, stapled to the top of their experiences, some that he had seen on multiple occasions. He had slept with two of them, one who got a part and one who desperately needed to.

His finger paused at Amanda's headshot, brunette locks and full lips. He slipped her out from the stack and read through. It wasn't anything special. She was a high school graduate, did modeling for various local boutiques, then was Eponine on Broadway. She met Mark through a mutual friend, the owner of a bar where she did tables for a while, who secretly introduced her as "bitchin' sex". Mark was opposed to such characterizations, so he tried to ignore the words that played like a tune in his head whenever he thought of her name. She was a good actress.

When he finally called her, she said, "Can you hold for a second?" and left him listening to Minuet. The wait made him nervous, though he felt he was in control of the situation.

"Still there?" she said, returning. Her voice was a refreshing transition from the music.

"This is Mark."

"Oh my god. I'm so sorry I made you wait, I was just getting changed—."

"Are you going somewhere?"

"No, just jogging, no big deal." She cleared her throat.

"Tell me this is a good call."

"I guess it's a good call." Mark smiled. "But that depends on if you're free for dinner at my place."

"Tonight?"

"That okay?"

"That sounds⋯⋯ perfect."

"Good."

"Did I get the part?"

"That, I will tell you during our wonderful dinner."

After hanging up, Mark felt as if her voice had kissed the inside of his ear. He checked his watch, confirmed that exactly three hours remained, and set his mind to planning the scene—champagne would be too forward, a bottle of wine and some steak would do.

But, like a stutter, his thoughts yanked back to the rat.

He couldn't think of anything worse than having a rat

around a woman. And it was inside his bedroom, of all places. Hamilton's joking remark returned and jittered inside his chest. "Fuck."

He called Amanda back to suggest a local restaurant. There was no answer. She had probably relocated to a salon by now.

The rat had to go.

The street was crowded; denizens scurried back and forth on the sidewalk and in and out of buildings in seemingly rehearsed uniform. They reminded Mark of a swarm of lemmings. Cutting through this human traffic, he tried to focus on a mental list of what he would need. He would combine Amanda shopping with rat shopping: a good bottle of wine, two steaks, some vegetables, and a hefty mousetrap. He had never noticed the odd store a block away from his apartment, where they sold everything from Yarmulkes to Nazi flags. That was exactly what was said in their yellow pages ad. When he called and asked about mousetraps, the first thing the guy said was, "How big?" and Mark knew it was the right place.

The store looked as if a warehouse had been barely shoved into its tiny space. There were heaps of things— tires, books, furniture—that didn't appear to be categorized or placed in any reasonable order. A small radio was playing *As Time Goes By,* but the sound was so damaged that Mark could barely make out the words.

"You the guy who called about a mousetrap, right?" The clerk was a heavyset Black man, with a bronze tanned face that made him look almost like a copper statue.

"How'd you know?"

"You're the first customer of the day."

He laughed in a baritone rumble.

"So is this a mouse or a rat?"

"A rat."

"Size?"

"Slightly taller than this." Mark gestured below the knee
with his hand.

"That's a big fucker."

"It's in my bedroom."

The man nodded wisely and walked through a door
behind the counter, continuing to nod to himself. He
returned shortly with a large mousetrap that looked like a
Japanese sandal.

"That's big," Mark noted.

"Big enough?"

"I sure hope so."

The man put the trap down on the counter and rolled up

his sleeves, like a doctor about to perform surgery, fetched his glasses from his breast pocket and put them on. "This is tricky, so listen carefully."

Mark leaned forward, but not too close.

"This thing right here, this is the bait pedal. And right here, this is the bow. This is what will clamp down—." He snapped his hand and yelled *crack,* startling Mark back. "And crush the shit out of it."

Mark pictured that. He breathed uneasily.

"Basically, put the bait inside this curl here at the end of the pedal, but you gotta put just a little, edible piece."

"Of cheese?"

"Yeah."

"Cheddar?"

"It doesn't matter. It's not gonna get to eat the fuckin' thing."

"That's true."

"Alright, just remove this staple, pull the bow back to here and lock it. Then put it next to a wall and wait. Put a newspaper sheet under it."

"Why?"

"The clamp is strong. You don't want guts all over your carpet." The man placed the trap inside a wooden box and handed it to Mark. It was heavier than he thought.

"Hey," Mark said. "You see Julius Caesar at Central Park?"

"Of course," the man said. "A brother plays Antony."

Mark smiled knowingly, "I did the casting for that." He said it so convincingly that he himself was convinced.

Mark repeated the directions in his head as he came out of the shop and headed down to the grocery store. The image of the clamp crushing the rat played over and over again, and while picking up the steaks, the clamp seemed to pinch the inside of his stomach. He tried to think of Amanda, but had a hard time juggling her and the rat, and once, unintentionally, he saw Amanda lying crushed under the clamp.

He approached his apartment with a bag full of groceries and the wooden box tucked carefully under his arm. Planning out the next two and a half hours, he kept his head low and watched his feet approach the front steps.

"Mark."

His feet came to a full stop.

May was standing at the top of the stairs, smoking a cigarette and tapping her foot. She looked significantly different from the night before. Her hair was let loose over her shoulders—not tied back—and the way she was poised made her look strangely tall. Mark couldn't think of a reaction, so he said, "What's up?"

She threw her cigarette down, stomped it out, then signaled with her head towards the entrance. "Can we go inside?"

Mark looked at his watch. "Yes. Yes, of course."

When they got inside his apartment, Mark feared that she might reach for the bedroom door, so he shuffled in front of her to block her out. Surprised, she took a step away and rolled her eyes up at him.

"Don't flatter yourself," she said. Her eyes dropped to his hand and saw the neck of the wine bottle sticking out of the grocery bag. "You got someone in there?"

"No." Mark realized it was ridiculous, but he said it anyway. "There's a rat in there."

She paused, then headed towards the livingroom, shaking her head. Mark followed her.

He placed the grocery bags, and the mousetrap, on the kitchenette counter and called out to May who sat on the couch without taking her coat off. "You want some water?" He had to peep out to see her nod.

When he returned with the glasses, she was staring at the cigarette butt on the table.

"I'm not planning on staying long." She picked up her glass, looked at the surface of the water for a moment, then put it back down without sipping. She kept her eyes away from him as she spoke. "I came to tell you that I'm leaving New York."

"What?"

"I'm going to school again. In Arizona."

"I don't understand. You didn't say anything last night." Mark sipped his cup of water and tried not to look at her either. In the corner of his eye, he saw May's hands rise up to her temples, her thin fingers pressing gently against them. She let out an extended sigh that sounded painfully cracked.

"Why'd you just leave this morning?" he asked.

"I shouldn't have been here this morning anyway, Mark," she said, her voice falling uncomfortably low.

"I'd like to talk about it."

"That's why I came over last night. But we ended up fucking, instead of talking. As always."

"That's not true." He put his glass down.

"We can still talk."

"I have nothing left to say. You talk."

"Alright." Mark checked his watch. "But not tonight. Definitely by the end of this week though."

"Listen to you," she said, suddenly turning to face him. "You're a complete asshole." She pushed her cup away.

"It's not what you think."

"I'm sure."

"I'm being serious. Hamilton's coming over for dinner."

May closed her eyes and tilted her head back against the couch. Mark saw something in her mascara that looked like a tear, but he wasn't sure.

"That's fine, Mark. You have a good evening."

She tried to get up, and Mark quickly leaned over, placing both his hands on her shoulders to keep her down. She grabbed him by the wrists and violently pushed him away, rising to her feet and almost tripping.

"Don't say anything," she said, her breaths picking up pace. "Don't even try to say anything." She trembled, so slightly that it was barely noticeable.

"May," he said, standing. "You're getting melodramatic."

"Shut up."

"We can work this out."

"Shut up, Mark."

She crouched her head down, her fingers pressing hard into her temples. She was shrinking, Mark thought, like a deflated balloon.

"You told me," she said, snapping her head up, "that if I couldn't trust your financial stability or even your fidelity, I could still believe in your potential."

Mark looked away, hoping that she would too. He couldn't recall ever saying such a thing, or using those very words at least.

"But where? Where is this fucking potential?" she continued. "You don't even talk about film anymore."

"Hey."

"Casting? This is what you went to school for? To fuck girls and barely pay rent?" She threw her hand into the air, gesturing at the bare livingroom.

"Stop."

"Have you even touched a camera once in the last year?"

"That's enough," Mark said, facing her. He took a step in her direction, and she drew back. "You can leave now."

She opened her mouth, as if to continue, but was stuck without a sound.

"I know what I'm doing," Mark said, turning away. "Don't tell me what to do."

In May's silence, the two of them could only hear the whirring of the air-conditioner, growing louder and louder like a thousand tiny voices giving birth to each other.

"This isn't you," she said.

Mark listened as his girlfriend's heels clicked along the floor, away from him and out of the apartment. He sat with his eyes closed and tried his best to ignore everything she had said. He imagined it as just another casting session, that a girl he never knew wanted a part very badly.

The clamp demanded surprising strength to pull back, and the force of its resistance made him wonder if it would actually cut the rat in half. After locking the bow down, he placed a piece of cheddar, from the chunk he had gotten to go with the wine, inside the curl of the bait pedal.

He checked his watch. Only an hour left. The steak was being prepared and all he needed now was to kill this rat quickly and cleanly. Handling the trap carefully in one palm, he opened the door slightly and scanned for the rat. It was nowhere visible, so he assumed that it was still under the bed. He opened the door a bit further and sent a newspaper sheet floating down to the carpet. Then he placed the trap softly, against the floor, careful as a father placing a child into a carriage. He looked at the mousetrap from behind the door, marveling at the skill with which it had been prepared.

After dressing up the coffee table with a sheet and finishing up preparations, Mark returned to the bedroom door. He checked his watch again: fifteen minutes. It had been a while since he checked up on the trap, and this time, he felt hopeful. He opened the door slightly and looked through. The trap was untouched. He closed the door, rushed over to the kitchenette, and returned with a bowl of crackers. He stood at the gap of the door, sitting with his legs crossed, eating crackers and awaiting the rat's death.

"Eat the cheese," he said. "You want to get out of here, don't you? Then eat the cheese."

The bowl was empty and the trap was still untouched when the doorbell rang. Mark stumbled up, stood confused for a moment, then threw the bowl into the room and shut the door. He straightened his shirt and hair, and looked at his bedroom door again, cursing under his breath. He felt like a boy waiting to meet his prom date without a corsage.

The rat made Mark nervous, but by Amanda's third glass of wine, he felt surprisingly comfortable with her. She wore a tight turtleneck sweater, her skirt hugging her thighs down to the knees where it met a pair of long, sleek boots. He had set the coffee table in the middle of the room, with two chairs facing each other, and the table was just low enough for a sliver of her thigh to be seen. When she asked about the part, Mark told her that it was between her and a woman named Valerie.

"It's ironic," he said.

She was smiling. "What is?"

"The first time you came over, you were the one who was

nervous." Mark sipped his glass. "But this time, I admit, I feel like you're casting me."

She laughed, and her laugh was different from all the other laughs in New York. It was sincere, like that of a tomboy, but also deliciously demure. "Maybe *I am* casting you." She laughed again.

Mark tried to place "bitchin' sex" like a subtitle under her. It didn't work.

They talked like this until the wine ran out, then she insisted on doing the dishes, immediately, saying, "I can't stand it when things are left undone." Afterwards, Mark poured her a mug of hot chocolate because she didn't like coffee, then the two of them sat together on the couch, talking about their first impressions of each other. Mark tried to be witty, wanting to hear her laugh over and over again.

"Can I ask you a personal question?" he asked.

"Sure." She placed a hand on his lap.

"Why didn't you go to college?"

He felt her hand tense up.

"I'm sorry, you don't have to discuss that."

"It's fine," she said. She forced a smile. "My father was sick at the time. He needed me."

Something in her eyes told Mark that her father was now dead, and Mark placed his hand over hers, feeling it press warmly against his lap. As if it had been rehearsed, she leaned into his body and kissed his cheek, then he turned towards her and kissed her lips. He felt the wine ride through his body and into his tongue.

"Let's go to your room," she whispered.

Mark paused. "We can't."

"Why not?"

He let out a breath, arching his body slightly away from

her.

"There's a rat in there," he said. "I know it sounds ridiculous but I've spent the entire day trying to get it out, but it's in there somewhere and I have this trap set up—."

She placed a finger over his lips and nodded. "The couch is fine." With her hands against his chest, she gently forced him down. She began unbuttoning his shirt and he felt his hands rise up with her sweater, pulling it over her neck and abandoning it at the side of the couch. She finished his shirt and kissed his chest, arching back again to undo her bra.

Falling back into him, she worked her way up to his ear and whispered, "*Screw* the rat."

Hearing her say that word—*rat*—sent a strange discomfort through his body. He kissed her neck and dipped his fingers in her hair, but it felt coarse at his fingertips, like touching salt.

"That dirty rat has no idea what he's missing," she whispered.

Mark pulled his fingers away. Amanda's body suddenly felt heavy, and he felt helplessly immobile, as if she was clamping him against the couch. Her hands reached down to work his zipper and he saw flashes of images in one blinding shot: forever awakening in an empty room, feeling around for a woman that would never be there.

"Wait," he said, easing her hand away. "I don't want to do this."

She paused, breathing heavy against his ear, then abruptly pulled away.

"Excuse me?"

Mark shifted away from her. "I don't want to do this."

She wrapped an arm around her chest and rose to her feet. "What do you mean you don't?" She almost sounded angry.

"Then why'd you call me here?"

Mark got up and placed a hand on her shoulder but she stepped away. "I'm sorry," he said. "I think you got the wrong idea about tonight."

She laughed, but this time it sounded hoarse. "It's alright," she said, leaning in again. "It's not the first time I've fucked to get a part."

Mark took a step back, putting his hand forward to distance her. The way she said *fucked* sounded exactly like the way she said *rat,* and he felt certain that this was all wrong.

"How could you say that?"

"Say what? You can't be new to this."

"That's not an excuse," he said, taking another step back. "Why do you do this? How can you do this?"

She stopped her approach. Her eyes turned to the abandoned plate of steak on the coffee table. Mark, unable to imagine what she was feeling, picked up her sweater from the floor and handed it to her. She took it without looking at him, then sat on the couch. She began to cry.

"I'm sorry," he said. "But there's no reason for you to do any of this."

She put on her sweater, straightened her skirt, then turned to face him. "I do this," she said, gesturing at the couch, "because the moment I spend being someone else on screen is better than the twenty-eight years I've spent being myself."

She sounded as if she were reciting a line. But she continued to cry as she turned away again, and Mark watched the back of her neck, stuck. He wondered if May would be home.

A loud crack broke the silence and Amanda snapped a hand to her chest in surprise. She turned to Mark, who shifted in confusion. Then, breaking, he rushed towards the bed-room.

He cracked open the door and slowly let his gaze drop to the trap near his feet. The rat was lying between the clamp and the wood base, its thick body violently crushed in the middle. The piece of cheese was lying next to the trap, as if it had been toppled away.

"That is fuckin' disgusting." Amanda was peering over his shoulder with a hand over her mouth.

Mark let the door swing open completely. He stared at the rat, grotesquely disfigured but clean, killed without much blood.

"It looks kinda peaceful," he said.

Matchbox

Winter, 1998

Six.

The father was napping on the sofa with his ailing hand on his bare stomach. The boy swiped a cigarette from the pack lying on the coffee table, picked up the rusty metal lighter, and tiptoed out on to the balcony. He carefully closed the glass door behind him and squatted, not sure of what to do but sure of what he had seen done. He held the cigarette at the corner of his mouth and lit a flame, watching it for a moment before actually lighting the cigarette. The tip picked up the burn and he turned and checked that his father was still sleeping. The first puff felt like a cotton strip slithering down his throat, and the boy coughed it out quickly. After a few more puffs he felt comfortable, so he leaned into the rails of the balcony with his back against the evening. He watched through the glass as his father's hand rocked gently against each swell of his belly, like a slow ferry at sea.

Eleven.

When the boy opened up his packed lunch, Mike spotted him from across the cafeteria, slapped a high-five to his friend and walked over. He snatched the sandwich from the boy's hand and snapped a bite out of it. Then, he dropped the rest of it back in the boy's Tupperware container, spat on it, and walked away. The boy watched as Mike retuned to his friends, who welcomed his gallant approach with rowdy approval. A girl sitting near them giggled, but the boy saw that it was actually just a smile. He got up, threw the torn sandwich in the trash can and walked out of the cafeteria.

Later, Mike caught the boy squatting and smoking under the tall grass at the edge of the school ground.

"What the fuck are you doing?"

Mike tipped the boy over with his foot and the cigarette dropped to the dirt. He saw the tip flicker as it fell, and wondered if it would cause a fire and burn everything up.

"Where'd you get that?"

"I swiped it from the old man."

Mike spat near the cigarette and considered the boy's answer. The smoke bled threads into the wind, and the boy felt that Mike didn't know what to do.

"I won't tell if you gimme a couple."

Fourteen.

The boy hadn't yet lit his cigarette when his father walked into the livingroom and spotted him squatting behind the glass.

"Shit, you said he was gone," Mike said, quickly throwing his cigarette into the yard. He began to rise but stopped and sat still.

The boy cupped his cigarette inside of his palm as his father walked over and opened the glass door. He wasn't sure if he had actually seen him with it, but the smoke from

Mike's first drag hung in the air and stung.

Mike got up, nodded a goodbye and walked into the livingroom and out of sight. The boy heard the door shut.

The father stepped onto the balcony and closed the door behind him. The boy imagined that he was going to get a beating.

"You smell guilty."

The father squatted next to him and fetched out a ruffled pack from his breast pocket. He slipped out a cigarette, placed it in his mouth, and all the while, the boy had no idea what was happening. The father turned to face him with the cigarette clinging to the bottom of his lip. "This look good?"

The boy felt the cigarette in his palm break. The tobacco bits soaked into sweat and made the skin of his hand feel like a wet sock. He shook his head.

The father tossed him the unlit cigarette and coughed,

then walked back inside, leaving the boy on the balcony.

At dinner, the boy's mother said that thieves beget thieves.

Seventeen.

The boy was buzzed as hell and admired the way Sandra looked in this condition. She was sitting next to Mike and some other guy, taking small sips of Mike's can of beer and listening to Mike talk about something.

Mike noticed that his friend was watching Sandra and brought her over to him. The girl was a bit tipsy, but her face wasn't red and she didn't look all that drunk. Mike set her down next to him on the couch and introduced them, but the boy didn't really say hi.

After Mike walked away it was very awkward because

Sandra kept staring into her beer can as if she had dropped something in it. The boy stared at her chest. She was wearing a tank top and he saw that she was quite big for her age. But she kept looking into her beer can and he wondered if he should do something or say something.

"What you got in there?" he said.

She smiled but didn't look at him. He watched as one of her fingers skated around the rim of the can.

"I'm sorry," he said. "I'm sorry but I haven't ever been drunk before and I think you're cool."

This time, the girl turned and faced him and smiled. The boy suddenly remembered a girl that had smiled at him a long time ago and wondered if it had been Sandra all along. But he wasn't sure, and really, it didn't matter because she was a beautiful girl and he was feeling like something was happening. "You're cute," she said.

Later, they went up to Mike's bedroom and made out for a while on the floor next to a pile of clothes. By then, the boy was feeling more and more sober and wondered if he should drink more. He held her awkwardly in his arms because she was slightly taller than him.

"You know, I thought you were going with Mike."

She rolled her eyes. "Mike's an asshole."

He didn't know what to say to that, so he, for no reason at all, told her that his father was sick with something bad. She said sorry but didn't really mean it, just like the boy, who didn't really mean to be felt sorry for.

Afterwards, they sat outside and shared a cigarette. The boy felt that it tasted better than usual.

Twenty-five.

With the phone against his ear, he took sips of water while looking out at the bay. A small boat was carving its way to coast. He told his mother that he never intended on quitting, but he never intended on starting either so it just sort of happened. She congratulated him and he could hear her relaying the news in a quieter voice. He closed his eyes and imagined his father lying on the couch at her side, slowly nodding his approval. But his father's belly was now shriveled like a prune, popping instead of swelling, his hand struggling to stay afloat.

After hanging up, he considered going for a jog. The boy was glad he had quit, but he had never wanted a cigarette more in his entire life.

A Glass of
Victory
Spring, 2000

I had imagined I would either be dead or extremely suc-cessful by now.

I sat at a table with Pat, watching his wife and kids finish their steak and begin their dessert. The wife smiled when she saw that I was watching. She had large, square teeth, like a mouthful of Chicklets gum. Their son looked like a magically shrunken version of Pat. Mini-Pat.

Pat was once the student council president, and I remember that not because I ran against him, but because he presently had the student council badge pinned against his blazer collar, as if he had never taken it off.

Pat: You put up a noble effort.

I watched mini-Pat struggle uncomfortably with his tie, strangled around a collar that was much too big for him. Pat's wife pinched his arm and he sat still, stealing a glance—a silent cry for help, perhaps—in my direction. I winked back.

It was painful to acknowledge that this was already the second reunion since those high school days, when you were either promising or making promises to be promising. I had never been promising, really, but I wasn't intending on making any more promises so I felt that I was okay. In fact I was presently pleased to find myself alienated from Pat's world which I now identified with an uncomfortable tie and a wife with big teeth.

When the server came around and gestured at my untouched steak, I nodded for him to take it away and gestured for another glass of wine.

"I'm sorry about Charlene."

I looked up from my almost empty glass and saw that Pat was trying to say something.

"I mean, if you don't want to talk about it, John—."

"But you'd like to talk about it, no?"

Pat's wife placed her hand on top of her husband's and gave a tiny but tight squeeze. Pat stole his hand away and looked at me as if I had interrupted an important lecture.

"I'd like to offer my condolences," he said. "I hope she'll be alright."

I finished my glass of wine and held it up between my eyes and Pat's family, observing them drowning into oblique shapes. I put the glass down and abruptly rose.

"You're a doctor, Pat. Vegetables don't get alright."

I turned and headed out of the gym, disguised for the night as a banquet hall, towards the men's room, fishing in my pocket for cigarettes. I imagined that mini-Pat was sitting dumfounded, turning to the omniscient head of the family to add: I hate vegetables, but tomatoes are okay.

A painfully old man was mopping the floor when I walked into the men's room. His blue overalls were dirtied with thick dust, complementing his hair and the mop being dragged around. It took me an awkward moment to recognize him as Carlos, the janitor who affectionately greeted me each schoolday morning. I suddenly felt the weight of age on my shoulders.

"You're still around, huh?" I said.

"Kids are dirty as ever." He finished up, seemingly prematurely, and placed his mop in the supply stall. He walked up closer, looked into my eyes, then patted me on the shoulder and walked out of the bathroom.

I sat inside a stall and lit a smoke. The wine was taking remarkable effect on my head, and I felt light-headed for the first time in a long time. I closed my eyes and tried to think of something pleasant but saw that Pat's student council badge was imprinted in my vision, its contours in faded light against black. I opened my eyes and stared above into the fluorescence, hoping to blind the image out.

I suddenly felt traces of the past floating back up from my lungs and feared that I would suffocate.

． ． ． ． ．

Pat won because he was a good orator. A natural politician. His father was a Senator somewhere and they were wealthy.

I closed my eyes again and tried to remember Pat's speech. It had been many years, and I could only remember the introduction.

Pat: Since there are only two candidates, recommending myself would be, unintentionally but nonetheless inevitably, an act that disdains a fellow classmate. Since most of you are already aware of my better traits, I would like to talk about my flaws and how you could help me correct them so that I may best serve you.

It was a clever way to begin a speech packed with witty quotes and anecdotes, a speech that was humble, funny, and inspiring all at once. It was well delivered, and I remember sitting on a chair at the side of the auditorium stage, hidden away from the crowd, nervousness growing in my chest as I watched his hand punch the air for impact. I don't remember much else of his speech, most likely because I was trying not to forget my own. Ironically, after the event, I remembered only his.

But as I recall, my speech was good too, almost as good as his, because I remember that the official announcement over the PA was: "Close call." Those two words lingered in my mind for months, and eventually throughout my entire senior year, drowning out the memory of my campaign, the rest of Pat's speech, and all of my own. Slowly, the phrase was stripped of the scenes associated with it, and by the end of my college days I was able to get over my loss to Pat. But I never forgot the words. Doused deep in my mind somewhere, they floated up at moments when I had no other words to offer. That's the way it was when I heard about my wife's car accident. I got the call from Charlene's friend and thought, "Close call".

It couldn't have been all about the speech. Pat must have won because he was more of an academic or because he was popular with some of the girls. There was this girl that I kinda liked—Mary—who was also thinking about running for president but decided to let Pat fill her share. I remember, right before Pat walked on stage, she ran over to the side where I was seated and whispered to him, "Good luck!" It was a very bad moment for me and I felt weakened by her, so I glared at her but she didn't see because she was watching Pat like a wife sending her husband into war.

When the announcement came over the PA, I was in biology class and some of the kids behind me whispered and giggled. I felt eyes scathing my back, and so I walked out of there as quickly as I could, sweaty as hell. The hallway I had walked for years felt narrower than before, and everything looked ridiculously disproportionate, as if the building was playing a joke on me for the whole world to laugh at. I sat inside the bathroom for hours until classes were dismissed, then waited an hour more for everyone to clear out so I could go home and shut myself up for the weekend.

When I got home I told my parents that it was a "close call", but they corrected me: "You lost." I repeated those two words—"Close call, close call, close call"—to myself the entire weekend, and often found myself blurting it out during dinner or even when I was watching TV alone. It was a close call, a few more votes my way would have changed the entire story, but it didn't matter. I had lost and it didn't seem to matter that I had *almost* won.

I flushed the cigarette down the toilet and laughed to myself, thinking how ridiculous it was that I was back in the bathroom, troubling over inconsequential details of a stupid, ridiculous high school election. Fuck it, I said under my breath.

When I walked out of the bathroom, Carlos was vacuuming the carpeted hallway leading me back towards the gym.

"They make you work this late?" I asked. The vacuum was loud, so I repeated louder, "You gotta work this late?"

He looked up and turned the vacuum off. "They make me work all the time." He shook his head a few times, and for a moment he looked like some kind of a sage, expressing great disapproval. "No work, no pay, you know how it is……"

"Yeah." I shrugged.

Suddenly, I remembered that Carlos was in the bathroom that day when my loss was announced, when I walked in, about to cry, hoping that I could be alone. He was doing his garbage bin rounds, and was just leaning over to pick out the bag when I entered. Almost as if he knew how I was feeling, he rushed out of the bathroom.

"I doubt you remember this," I said. "That time I walked into the bathroom and I was about to cry? You were······ You know, doing garbage bin rounds?"

Carlos stood, considering, then nodded.

"You do?"

"My job is routine," he said. "You remember little differences."

I felt a strange glee at the knowledge that someone shared that memory, something that had been confined to me for so long.

"You know," I said. "I lost a pretty important election that day."

Carlos nodded slowly, and I wondered if he knew what I was talking about. "You were sad," he said. "I asked you something and you didn't answer."

"I was just too sad to talk," I said. Then I saluted him, which was something I had never done before but probably did because I was feeling slightly drunk. I turned and headed back towards then gym, but feeling like I was selling Carlos short on something, I immediately turned back and asked, "What did you ask?"

Carlos tilted his head up at the ceiling, looking as if he was digging through infinite mounds of memory. "Ah," he said. "I found something of yours in the trash bin, so I asked you if you wanted it."

"What was it?"

"It was a bunch of papers, small memos. But they had your name on it, so I thought it was in there by mistake. No big deal, I guess."

．　．　．　．　．

Pat's wife was still eating her dessert when I returned to my seat. Pat was standing two tables down, leaning into a crowd of faces. I watched the badge on his blazer pop up and down with each exaggerated comment he was making.

I got up, walked over to his wife and picked up her glass of wine. She looked up confused and watched as I walked over to where Pat was orating and threw my arm around his shoulder. He flinched in my grasp and the crowd before him looked up, shocked out of what I saw as complete boredom.

"To Pat!" I said, throwing my glass up into the air.

The crowd nervously handled their glasses and did the same. I could feel Pat heat up with discomfort.

"Student council president Pat!" I yelled, this time attracting almost everyone in the gym. I downed the wine like a thirsty teenager and dropped the empty glass on the table. Some cheers could be heard from across the gym, but 'everything was silenced when I maneuvered Pat into a menacing headlock and kneed him in the stomach. But Pat was stronger than I thought, and slowly, painfully, he forced himself out of my grip and shoved me away. I fell hard into the table and closed my eyes quickly as everything around me seemed to collapse, accompanied by the sick music of breaking glass and jumbled phrases.

"You⋯⋯ You crazy fuck," Pat said, pulling himself together.

I opened one of my eyes and saw the whirl of bodies, shuffling in panic and confusion. Pat's wife was clinging to Pat's arm, with her mouth wide open, full of Chicklets.

Amidst the confusion, I had a moment of clarity, and it occurred to me that this was the first time I had ever heard

Pat curse. I looked up to see him fix his attire, shaken. His student council badge was no longer visible; it must have fallen off during the conflict.

"Goddamn, that was a close call," Pat said, searching around the faces for approval.

I looked down at my hand and saw that I was firmly gripping his student council badge. I closed my eyes and laughed deeply, for the first time in many years.

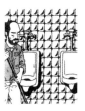

The Walls of Our World
Spring, 2001

A conversation with Sandra is like swimming in a Pollock painting: words, expressions and hands flutter and mix, raw and brilliant. She makes speech purely physical. I lose the meaning of her sentences and throw myself into the storm of her lips.

But, I remind myself, I have a job to do.

"Tell me about last Saturday," I say. "Tell me."

Her eyes widen in excitement as if she has anticipated

this very question, this chance to expose herself. Like a budding actress speaking her debut lines, she wets her lips with her tongue and draws in a long breath that threatens to inhale the whole room.

"I danced and danced, toes and heels pecking the earth like birds feeding," she answers.

Sandra always speaks like this: poetry at the speed of a subway train.

"Where was this?" I ask, watching nothing but her lips.

"In the rain. I danced between the strips of rain."

"This was Saturday?"

"Yes."

"Are you sure, Sandra? It didn't rain on Saturday."

"It didn't rain for you, maybe, but it always rains for me. The sky shatters and rains shards of glass."

"That sounds very painful."

"No, it sounds beautiful."

Everything she says is beautiful. Her lips are a fountain with words brimming; I, with my hands cupped, wait for them to overflow.

I glance over at the white booklet laid neatly on the top right-hand corner of my desk. A handbook for psychiatrists and their patients: *Therapy does not involve sex.* Warning signs. But when Sandra speaks, I forget about the roles we are paid to play.

"Rescue me," I say.

"What?"

Let's dance together, speak together, compose sentences that will bridge the space between my chair and your couch, between my sterile white dress shirt and your unbuttoned blouse.

"Nothing," I hurriedly say.

"You can have me," she says.

"What?"

"You can have me and take me wherever you want."

Her words make the marble pillars fall; office walls cave in; phone numbers disappear from the rolodex; and appointment cards burn to cinder, leaving nothing but Sandra and I, hand in hand, waiting to rescue each other. But it's too late for either of us to be saved.

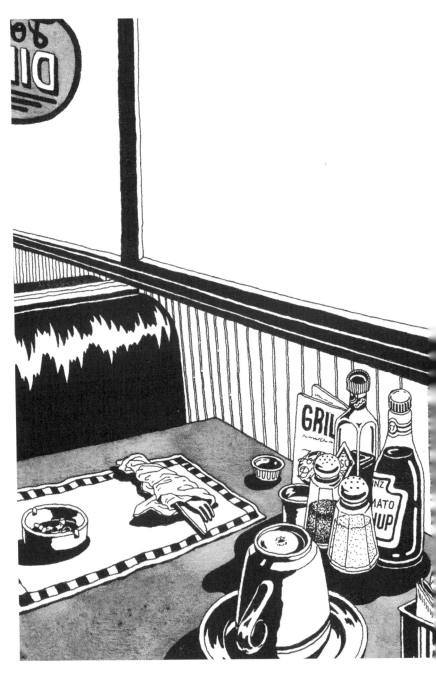

Hate Crime
Winter, 2000

Junseok paused briefly but deliberately at the entrance of the diner, observing his reflection against the glass door. *Johnny's Diner* was wiped across his face, his hair combed neatly to the side to expose his broad forehead and thick black eyebrows. He squinted to concentrate on his teeth, scanning for any traces of red pepper or yellow egg from his udon lunch at his grandmother's. No traces. Clean and white as ever.

He stepped into the diner and waved a two-fingered greeting to Johnny behind the counter. A rock song was playing from the jukebox by the door, filling the air above him. He couldn't identify it, but it sounded like something from the fifties. It blended well with the warm, familiar smell of grilled cheese and coffee at the counter.

"How's it?" Junseok asked, leaning against a stool.

"Busy," Johnny said. He was flipping through a stack of memo pads. Receipts. "What you been up to, kid? Haven't seen you here in weeks."

"I, too, have been busy. College stuff won't let me out of my room."

"Well," he said, smiling, "I wouldn't know how that is. But I know you're damned smart, so you should be busy with that kind of thing."

"Yep."

"What about your girl?"

"She's been busy too, apparently."

Junseok smiled and walked away from the counter to the corner seats, where he and Margaret normally sat. He laid a menu open in front of him, then checked his watch. She was late, and he wondered if it would be reasonable to order anything at all.

He fetched today's paper from the rack next to the door and returned to his seat. Just as he turned to the funny pages, he heard the tiny bell at the entrance ring. Margaret. She was wearing a raincoat for some reason, though it hadn't rained in almost a week. Junseok watched patiently as she exchanged a few words with Johnny. He let her find him.

"Sorry," she said, finally sitting down, across from him. She didn't say anything more, though it would have been appropriate. Instead, she quickly scanned the specials, then turned and yelled for a roast beef sandwich to Johnny. "You want anything?" she said, turning back.

Junseok shook his head and closed his menu and put it to the side. He turned back to the comic strips, not really reading but trying his best to look at something other than her face.

"I'm really sorry about being late. You want to do this some other time?"

Without looking up, he said, "It's fine."

He had originally planned this to be a lot easier. For the past three days, he wrote it out like a play in his mind, revising what he would say, and sometimes reconfiguring what she would say, just so that he would be prepared for all possibilities. But now he was forgetting his lines.

"There isn't really much to say," she said.

Junseok looked up, slightly relieved, but bitter, that she was starting the conversation.

"I understand that you must hate me. I can't stop you from feeling that. But I want you to know that this isn't something I planned."

"Margaret," he said, taking a breath. "That doesn't change a damned thing."

She looked down at the table, almost shamefully.

"I know."

"Margaret Atkinson. Intelligent, beautiful, whatever. I'm not surprised." He was finally remembering what he had prepared.

"What's that supposed to mean?"

"You know, I'm just this boring guy who's gonna graduate, work, work, work, until I can do surgery. Scalpels versus baseballs, I don't know. I just don't know."

"He plays basketball." She quickly took her eyes away again. It was the wrong thing to say.

"Basketball, football, soccer, skateboarding, whatever. I'm boring."

"No, you're not."

"I'm dull. Bland."

"You're wonderful."

She stared back with clear blue eyes and a shy smile, her brunette locks falling just above her cheekbones. It was this sincere, unblemished face that he had fallen in love with so long ago.

She was throwing a damned curveball.

"Then why the hell are you going off with that jock?"

"It's not because you're not wonderful. You really are. Things just happened this way."

"Forget it. I'm going to the men's room."

Junseok got up and stomped away from her towards the bathroom. He didn't really need to go, but there was nowhere to turn.

He wet a paper towel and placed it against his brow, then wiped it across both of his cheeks, pushing the wetness against his skin in slow, pained massages. Wonderful, she says. I'm wonderful. I'm wonderful and she wants to leave me to go with a sweaty guy who'll shoot basketballs and fuck her brains out on the weekends. That's wonderful. He wet another paper towel and massaged his face again. He was sweating.

When he returned to the table, Margaret was reading something from the newspaper. She had left the funny pages on his side.

"This is so wrong," she said, squinting her whole face at the paper. "You won't believe how wrong this is."

"What? War?"

"Listen to this: Tragedy befell the Vietnamese community on Jan 29, 1996, when Thien Minh Ly, a 24-year old Vietnamese man and former graduate of UCLA, was murdered while rollerblading in his Tustin hometown high school tennis court." She read it very slowly and carefully, enunciating every syllable as if she were reading a poem.

"It's a sick world."

"Yes, but it's worse than you think. He was found with hundreds of stab wounds, and his throat was slit too."

"That's fucked up."

"Listen to this: Police arrested Gunner Lindberg, age 21, and Dominic Christopher, age 17, after discovering a letter that Lindberg had written to a former prison inmate in New Mexico. The letter contained graphic details about the murder, as well as the writer's apparent insouciance about the whole incident. Sandwiched between birthday plans, news about a friend's baby, and talk about the need for a new tattoo was this boastful account of what happened the night of Jan 29th."

"Let me see that."

Junseok grabbed the paper from her and found the killer's words:

Oh I killed a jap a while ago I stabbed him to Death at Tustin High school I walked up to him Dominic was with me and I seen this guy Roller blading and I had a knife. We walk in the tennis court where he was I walked up to him. Dominic was right there I walked right up to him and he was scared I looked at him and said 'Oh I thought I knew you' and he got happy that he wasn't gonna get jumped. Then I hit him......

It was grammatically horrendous, and Junseok wondered why they hadn't edited it.

I stomped on his head 3 times and each time said 'Stop looking at me' then he was kinda knocked out Dazzed then I stabbed him in the side about 7 or 8 times he rolled over a little so I stabbed his back out 18 or 19 times then he layed flat and I slit one side of his throught on his jugular vain. Oh, the sounds the guy was making were like Uhhh. then Dominic said 'do it again' and I said 'I already Did. Dude. 'Ya, Do it again' so I cut his other jugular vain, and Dominic said 'Kill him Do it again' and I said 'he's already Dead' Dominic Said 'Stab him in the heart' So I stabbed him about 20 or 21 times in the heart⋯⋯ Then I wanted to go back and look, so we Did and he was dieing just then taking in some bloody gasps of air so I nidged his face with my

shoe a few times, then I told Dominic to kick him, so he
kicked the fuck out of his face and he still has blood on his
Shoes all over······ then I ditched the knife, after whiping it
clean onto the side of the 5 freeway······ here's the clippings
from the newspaper we were on all the channels.

When he finished, Junseok looked up at Margaret who
was holding a hand against her chest and squinting her face
so hard that he feared she would cry.

"It's a hate crime," she said.

Junseok nodded and looked back down at the article.

Oh I killed a jap a while ago I stabbed him to Death.

He looked at the word "jap" and felt dirty and embarrassed. "These guys are fucking crazy. This guy, this guy, he

didn't even do anything. And look at this grammar. Why didn't the paper edit any of this?"

"It is *so* wrong."

"The dead guy, it says here that he just got his Master's in physiology and biophysics."

"I can't understand why anyone would do that."

"They fucking stabbed him like a hundred times. He must have been unrecognizable."

"Think about the family. His mother."

"'The Tustin police seemed reluctant to publicize the racial implications of the crime. For instance, the Tustin Weekly omitted the words—I killed a jap—in their rendition of Lindberg's letter.' Wait, they *did* edit it. I don't get it. Why the hell would they do that?"

"I'm so sorry."

Junseok looked up from the article. Margaret held out a

hand and placed it on top of his. He couldn't tell if it was trembling because his own hand was shaking pretty badly now.

"Why are you sorry?"

"Because, because you're Korean."

"So?"

"He was one of your people."

Junseok snatched his hand away from her. He quickly shoved it under the table.

"I'm Korean-American," he said.

"But still."

"Still what? This guy was Vietnamese. How is he one of *my* people?"

"Well, both of you are Asians."

Junseok stared back at her sincere eyes, then at his hand under the table. He wanted desperately to explain how nonsensical her comment was, but instead, he folded up the paper slowly and carefully. Tucking it under his arm, he got up, and without saying anything to her, walked towards the exit. She called from behind, but he walked on, feeling the dirtiness expand inside him like a large flower. Each step quickened until he was running, running out the door and into the street, running past people and cars, running without the faintest idea of what he was running from, to a place that he couldn't possibly picture in his mind.

Coup de Grace
Spring, 2001

Richmond Walker felt that his life had been derailed from greatness; he had inadvertently fallen from the ring into a loveless marriage and an unexpectedly large inheritance that landed him here, at the wheel of a Benz, with a nine-year old son in the backseat reading an inconsequential novel about a woman's dinner party.

"That book is garbage," he said.

Jacob Walker looked up from his book, his thick-rimmed

glasses hanging precariously against a short noodle of a nose. He was wearing his dull-gray prep-school uniform, as his father had prescribed. The insignia on the breast pocket, a shield with the school's motto—*Sine Timore, Aut Favore*—was exactly half the span of his chest.

"Hemingway. Now there's a writer," Richmond continued. "And a boxer, like I was. Your teacher doesn't like him, does she?"

Jacob closed the book, placed it neatly on his lap, and turned to face out the window. He hadn't seen the outside world for the entire ride, and now, as the car turned on to Malcolm X Boulevard, Jacob felt the roots of his hair dig like a thousand pins into his scalp.

"Is this where Uncle Frank lives?" he asked, desperately gripping *Mrs. Dalloway* with frail, straw-like fingers.

The car stopped abruptly at an ill-lit sidewalk, a line of

broken-down shops stretching into the darkness ahead of them. Bright, neon *Closed* signs danced like giant fireflies before Jacob's eyes.

Richmond fixed his silver cufflinks, picked off a dot of lint from his tux, and turned, smiling, to face his son, shriveled against the black leather seat.

"Your mother's incessant socializing has forced this upon us," he said, noting the pleasantness of his own authoritative tone. "Damn her for making me attend these silly, inconsequential parties."

Jacob nodded, fear colliding with awe and confusion. He searchingly scanned the world outside, hearing the hollow symphony of the Harlem street—low voices and distant engines—scratching gently against the glass wall that protected him.

"No, father," he mumbled. "Please."

"Look at you," Richmond mocked, almost yelling, "Fearful of a challenge. You, a prizefighter's son?"

"Please."

"I'll be back to pick you up in exactly two hours. You have your blazer on so you won't freeze to death."

An aged Black man, with layers of fish-scales for a face, knocked at Jacob's window with a soup can. His bloodshot eyes fluttered like searchlights around the elegant interior of the car.

"Father, please," Jacob muttered, desperately, shrinking away from the man at the window.

"You're not scared of being alone, are you? Please don't tell me you're scared of being independent. Answer me, Jacob. Are you scared of being alone on the street for two fuckin' hours?"

"Please let me go with you."

Richmond leaned over and opened the door for his son. Then, with the back of his hand, he slapped Jacob's face with a rapid snap, knocking his glasses onto the curb. His son's cheek turned blood red, like a hot coal.

The old man outside took a few steps back and waited expectantly, tapping his can with a finger.

. . . . .

Valerie Walker carried her beauty as a soldier carries a medic kit, concealing a tiny tube of perfume between her thigh and the elastic grip of her stockings. Her life had been a relay of obsessions: weight-loss ran through her high-school years, breast enlargements through college, until, recently, the baton was passed to intoxicating scents. She feared odors to the point that, when she would flip through the *Times* or the *New Yorker*, she shuddered at words like "odious" or "ode".

"It's just such a hassle for Frank," she said, stepping into the car. "Jacob's old enough to take care of himself now, don't you think?"

Her scent, large flowers smashed to a pulp, shot against Richmond's face like an airbag.

"I didn't leave him with Frank. I left him with a friend."

"Who?"

"A friend of mine. He's Black."

Valerie squinted at him with sharp aversion. She personally had not ever known a Black person, or any other "colored" person for that matter; her wealth afforded her the privilege of making such encounters as rare as spotting pandas anywhere outside of a zoo.

"Since when do you have a Black friend?" she asked,

nervously.

"I have plenty of Black friends. I was a boxer for criss-akes."

The answer deadened the air, and Valerie decided that her husband was again in one of his strange and undefined moments of ill will.

Richmond lit a cigarette and rolled down the window. He had only recently started smoking, wrapping himself with an odor that nibbled tauntingly at her senses.

Valerie sat silently for the rest of the ride to "Penny" Vain's mansion, remembering the Richmond she had met in her youth: a reticent young man whose resume outdid anything on his five-foot seven frame. It was a marriage between households, a holy business merger, an "I do" of monetary value. "Marriage is learning to love the furniture more than the home," her mother said, the night before the wedding. She was right. Richmond's inheritance afforded her the benefits of a marriage without the nagging responsibilities of a wife and mother. It thus didn't bother Valerie that after so many years she knew only anecdotes, nothing at all really, of her husband or her son; they existed in a private, secretive world she cared little for. Such detachment was the currency of their lives together.

Still, Valerie thought, there were times, rare moments of irrationality, when she longed for something else, something less practical or tangible, but—"I never knew you were a boxer," she remarked, not looking at Richmond.

. . . . .

Penny Vain's atrium, where Richmond bunkered himself with a fern and an old couple, was a menagerie of business cards and cocktails. His wife was somewhere on the second or third floor, he guessed, streaming through an ocean of incessant chatter about sons and daughters. The aging husband standing uncomfortably close to him had a diseased hand that shook to control his glass.

"You do nothing?" the old man asked.

"Absolutely nothing," Richmond repeated.

"He must have been in computers," the man's wife offered. "They retire early."

"I was a boxer." Richmond held up a fist, exposing a thick scar on one of his knuckles. "This one's from a street brawl."

The old man nodded courteously, then nudged his wife with an elbow. The couple harmonized an *it was nice meeting you* and walked away.

Richmond, relieved, checked his watch and calculated the

amount of time left before his rendezvous with Jacob.

Leaving his son in Harlem was an unexpected development, but a satisfying one nonetheless. Last week, he discovered that Frank had been pampering Jacob instead of toughening him up. Giving him caviar and sonnets. Ridiculous.

"Richmond Walker!" Penny roared from across the atrium, flanked by Dr. Joseph Lee and, to his mild surprise, Valerie. They approached slowly and galiantly like synchronized chess pieces. "We see you hiding!"

Richmond downed the rest of his scotch and stepped further behind the fern. "Fuck," he said under his breath.

"Hide and go seek?" Penny asked, tauntingly, placing a hand on his shoulder.

"Funny," he replied, shrugging the hand off. "I see that you're not dead yet."

"Ooh, this man needs something stronger than a scotch." Penny looked to his companions for a laugh, but they were frozen in discomfort. "Where's Jacob?"

"My son," Richmond said, drawing his breath, "is at a football practice."

"What?" Valerie interjected, leaning in. Then, seeing that there was no point in trying to *reason* with her husband, she agreed. "I must attend Mrs. Busby upstairs," she said suddenly, excusing herself with a nod.

Penny, as if taking an acting cue, wrapped an arm around her and said, "Let me take you to her. Remember, at my party, a woman unattended by me is *pennyless*." With that, he led her off, laughing weakly.

Penny, short for Penitent, was the owner of a travel agency for the wealthy, specializing in adventure packages for men and women who had wasted their adventurous years in labs, banks, and cubicles. He saw himself as New York's guru of free spirit.

"That man is a fucking asshole," Richmond said, now alone with Joseph. "I'd take him down any day."

"Why the hell have you been skipping your appointments, Rich?"

Richmond crunched his brow and held an accusatory finger up to Joseph's face. "Do you talk like this to all your patients?"

"You're inconsiderate. Cancel the appointments, at least."

"I installed a punching bag in the basement. I'm training again. Besides, I don't need you anymore."

"You're not the judge of that, unfortunately."

"And you are?"

"Tomorrow, 5pm. I'll see you in my office. For the last time, if you please."

Just then, the ringer on Richmond's cell-phone went off, and nearly every hand in the atrium reached for its counterpart pocket. He held a hand up to Joseph to freeze the conversation and answered the phone.

"Sir, are you Jacob's father?" the voice, a young woman's, asked in desperation.

"Who are you?"

"I'm looking for Mr. Walker."

"And who are you?"

"I'm Jacob's English teacher."

Richmond cupped the phone and turned his back to Joseph. "How did you get this number?"

"Is this Mr. Walker? Jacob's father?"

"How the hell did you get this number?"

"Sir, Jacob's here with me. He seems to be in quite a spell. He called me from a payphone in Harlem."

"A spell?"

"He was sitting on the curb of a street in his uniform. He won't say why he was there. He urinated in his pants, sir."

"Fuck," he said, for the second time in the evening.

. . . . .

Richmond, Valerie, Jacob, and Lori the English teacher, stood at the doorway of the Walker home, exchanging last words. The young woman had insisted on driving separately with Jacob, to "clarify" certain things. Richmond was ashamed; his son had cried for nearly an hour in the teacher's shabby apartment in East Village, and, even now, was slightly sniffling.

"You must be very proud to have a son like Jacob," she said, not looking at Richmond but at everyone else.

"For what?" Richmond asked, annoyed that she still had things to say.

"He won a creative writing competition," she said, confused. "He didn't tell you?"

"How nice," Valerie remarked, nodding. "He reads *all* the time."

"Anyone can win a creative writing competition," Richmond added. "But it ain't no champion belt."

Lori stared at Richmond's face, shocked that the man was dead serious. She realized that there was something of a macabre nature under his innocuous, well-groomed mask. "May I speak to you in private, sir?"

Valerie, who was annoyed that the night had been cut short, gladly led Jacob into the house and slammed the door. The night was cold but artificially still, as it always was in this neighborhood.

"Allow me to be forward with you, sir," Lori said, looking directly into his eyes for the first time. "There is a nasty bruise on Jacob's cheek, and a few remnants on his arms."

"Those are nothing."

"Excuse me?"

"Go on."

After an uncomfortable pause, she continued.

"You wouldn't happen to know how they got there?"

"No."

"Are you sure?"

"Don't second-guess me, young lady."

"Sir, you're not that much older than I am."

"I said, no."

She took a step back, still staring, as if to get a bigger picture. "Jacob says he fell, repeatedly. That, to me, is ridiculous."

"Your assumptions, to me, are ridiculous. Get to your point."

"He does get bullied frequently," she said, sighing. "There are kids at school that like to pick on him simply because he's······ unique."

"He can't even defend himself."

"He shouldn't have to, sir." She drew a deep, nervous breath and eyed him in disapproval.

"I care about your son very much. He's a prodigy."

"I'm sure that means a lot."

"It does. That competition he won," she said, lips breaking into a tilted smile, "was for college students." Her eyes flared, expecting that this bit of information would tip the man over to her side.

"I am now certain," Richmond said, as absolutely as he could, "that America's education system celebrates cowards instead of men."

Lori cowered back, paused, then exhaled in disbelief. "You're a horrible person." She stepped back quickly and hurried to her car, stupefied by the words of this demigod of a man. His voice, his door, his house, and the entire New York suburb threatened to swallow her world of points of views, polished sentences, and denouements.

When Richmond entered the house, Valerie was sitting at the foot of the stairs with her face planted in her hands. She was silently sobbing, broken breaths muffled by her palms. As he walked past her, she looked up; to his surprise, she was smiling uncontrollably.

"I'm in love with Penny Vain," she said.

Jacob was lying in bed with a novel sprawled open against his stomach. Richmond, eyeing his son's embarrassingly feminine hands, tapped him awake with a flick to his forehead.

"You like to make up stories?" he asked, softly. "You like imagined worlds where you can be what you're not?"

Jacob nodded slowly.

"Are you a hero in your stories, Jacob? Because you're certainly not a hero in the real world, are you?"

"No, I'm not," he answered.

"Real men don't make up stories, Jacob. Real men are *real*." Richmond grabbed his son's arm and pulled him up to a sitting position. "Your teacher tells me about bullies. You don't like bullies, do you?"

Jacob shook his head.

"You need to defend yourself, Jacob. All great men defend themselves. Get up."

Jacob slipped out of bed and stood with knees rattling.

"You hate me, don't you?"

"No."

"Yes you do."

"I don't."

"Even after what I did to you today?"

Jacob, keeping his head low, his eyes fixed at his father's enormous toes, answered with complete silence.

"I bullied you today," Richmond continued. "I hurt you, I dealt the first blow, so you need to defend yourself. Do you want to be a coward for the rest of your life?"

Jacob didn't, couldn't, respond.

"No. No, you don't. You don't want to waste your existence offending no one and defending nothing, do you?"

Jacob, confused, muttered a quiet *no*.

"Then defend yourself," Richmond repeated.

In a sudden, violent sweep, he planted his fist into Jacob's chest, flattening his son against the floor. Jacob writhed in pain, gasping for breath like a fish torn out of water.

"Come on, Jacob, defend yourself." Richmond picked up his son and held him till he could stand on his own feet. Looking directly into his eyes, like a coach to his beloved champion, he said, "Be a real man." With that, another blow to the chest sent Jacob back to the floor.

After five repeated knockouts, Richmond felt shame flood his insides like polluted water. This was the son of a prizefighter, the grandson of a war hero: a writer who probably couldn't even break a pencil.

"Defend yourself, goddamit!" Richmond yelled.

Jacob was barely standing, his head swinging like a pendulum.

Richmond, disgraced, delivered his coup de grace, bringing his fist over the top of his son's head.

·　·　·　·　·

Valerie, lying in bed with eyes skating against the ceiling, felt an uncontrollable sensation coursing through her veins. Emotion. She was in love with Penny Vain; nothing, not even her dead mother, could cork her passion shut. It was groundbreaking, an epiphany as someone had once called it: she was, for the first time in her life, not afraid to lose the house, the carpet, the shared bank account. Penny was all she wanted. Though it would be quite a migraine—the divorce, Jacob—tomorrow night, she would allow Penny's advances to unwrap her like a gift box.

Downstairs in his study, Richmond sat brooding, a couple of glasses of whiskey resting like paperweights against the bottom of his stomach. Everything, utterly every single one of his attempts, had failed. Four months of secret household bootcamps—fighting drills, football lessons, cursing sessions—had been completely futile. Jacob was a first-rate coward. If he couldn't defend himself, how could he defend his fellow men, his father, or his country?

He opened the bottom of his oak executive's desk—once his father's—where a shiny silver pistol lay in a velvet case. He picked it up and examined his contorted reflection against the barrel. It was unloaded, of course. He owned no bullets and had never planned to; the gun was a relic from the fortune he inherited from his father. He put the gun back in the velvet case and sat still, trying to wave off memories of his father that descended over his skin like a cocoon.

. . . . .

It rained the next afternoon, thick threads of water crack-
ing like tiny cymbals against the window.

"Your son is not a coward," Dr. Joseph Lee said, staring
at his college-buddy-turned-patient Richmond. "He's like
every other boy at the age of nine. At least he's not a bully."

"Is that supposed to make me feel better?" Richmond
inquired, shocked at his friend's naiveté. "I *want* him to be a
bully."

"Why? Bullies are the real cowards of this world, you
know."

Richmond stared back in confusion. "Perhaps you and I
need to switch seats here."

"Cowards, I believe, are people who are afraid to embrace what they want or need in a natural, honest way. Bullies, for example, replace their need for attention or care with irrational violence," Joseph said, monotonously. "Your son is not a coward, he's just shy, timid, introverted."

"This is why I don't need you anymore," Richmond abruptly said, getting up from his seat. "You're a fucking quack, Joe. You're a fucking quack hustling terms and labels because you can't be on the street pushing the real thing."

"Sit down, Rich."

Richmond waved him off and continued to stand.

"Let's talk about you," Joseph started again, clearing his throat. "I'm curious about these riddles you've been throwing at me."

"What riddles?"

"About your father being in the Korean War. I don't recall you ever mentioning that before."

"How's that a riddle?"

Joseph checked his notes. "Because you told me, roughly five months ago, that your father was never in that war."

"That's not possible."

"That is what's recorded, Rich."

"Fuck you, Joe," he said, backing up a step. "Don't call me a liar."

"I never called you that."

"That's what you're trying to say."

"No—."

"If you think I'm a liar, just call me that. Don't be such a fucking coward about it."

"Don't call me a coward," Joseph said, rising from his chair and joining Richmond at eye-level. "I'm trying to help you."

"You're a coward like Penny Vain, who, may I add, is sleeping with my wife."

"I know about that."

"You do?"

"Everyone in New York knows," Joseph said, waving his hands in the air. "You've been too self-involved to see what's happening all around you."

Richmond paced the large office, looking from the framed paintings on the wall to the contents on Joseph's oppressively large desk: a rolodex, an institutional-looking phone, and a thick file with a white label that read *Richmond J. Walker.*

"Look at the cowardly world you've built, Joe."

"We are all cowards in a way."

"I am not a coward," Richmond said, pointing a menacing finger in his friend's direction.

"I was a prizefighter in my youth."

"Rich, you were never a prizefighter······ You were never a boxer."

"What are you talking about?" Richmond yelled, stepping back to add distance between the two.

"Rich, stop."

"What the fuck are you saying? Are you insane?"

"Rich, you never boxed a single round in your life."

Richmond placed a hand against the wall to steady himself. "You're out of your mind."

"It's alright. You've had a difficult life," Joe said, calmly approaching Richmond. "I understand that things aren't lucid."

"You're a liar."

"It's all recorded in that file over there, Rich. Your father hurt you, but you can't let him control the rest of your life."

"That's a lie," he said, fumbling his words.

"My father was a great man. He was a war hero, not a coward like you."

"No, Rich. You're the coward," he said, shaking his head.

The word *coward*, like an unexpected blow to the chest, pressed Richmond against the wall. Joseph's eyes fell like a heavy anchor to the floor; he realized that he had crossed major professional boundaries. But he felt liberated. Out of the box. Free to speak like a real man.

"I'm sorry, but you're not the same person who came to see me a year ago, Rich. I can't help you anymore."

In a sudden, violent slice, Richmond's fist cut through the thick air of the office and planted itself just below Joseph's cheekbone. Joseph fell over on his back, landing with a thud against the carpeted floor.

"I am not a coward, you motherfucker."

Richmond picked up his file from Joseph's desk and rushed out of the room, leaving his old friend and doctor behind in his glass house of a world, flat on the broken floor.

Stepping onto the street, Richmond Walker held his file tight in his grip and cried for the first time in years.

· · · · ·

Valerie adored her daily trips to the salon, where a smorgasbord of pleasantries awaited her like a bouquet of butlers. As Janice, her pregnant stylist, worked large curls into her hair, she imagined that the entire universe would change tonight, and that, like the life of a musical heroine from the '50s, all voices would sing and sigh to the sparkle of her evening.

I'm in love, she sang in her head, off-key.

She looked at Janice's swelled stomach in the mirror and wondered what the lives of other women must be like. She imagined dirty pantyhose, unwashed coffee mugs and carpet stains.

"Janice, darling, hurry," an old lady called out from the waiting area. "I've been waiting for almost ten minutes."

The horribly aging woman, red hair fluffed like the end of a duster, continued reading her magazine. Women like this suffocated Valerie. Women like this, she thought, had insides like used vacuum bags.

"Janice," she called out again. Like an uncultured animal in an opera, she spoke at an utterly uncivilized volume. "It's a tragedy, a modern-day tragedy."

"What is?" Janice asked.

"Penitent Vain has gone bankrupt," she answered, shaking her head.

"What?" Valerie almost snapped her neck.

"You're kidding," Janice answered, matter-of-factly. "That's terrible."

"Yes, terrible, isn't it?" the lady chimed in, eyes still planted in her magazine. "It's all over the papers as well."

Valerie erupted out of her seat, pushing aside Janice's hands.

"Dear, what's wrong?" Janice asked, stepping away and shielding her stomach.

With hands shaking uncontrollably, breaths spitting out like tiny pellets, Valerie fetched a wad of tens from her purse and placed it on her empty seat. Only one side of her head had curls, but like a fugitive, she ran out of the salon, nails digging into her palms.

Outside, she crouched before a metal rack haphazardly

filled with the local community paper. Picking one out, she spread it open on the sidewalk, and like a mother searching for a lost child, pored over the newsprint with tear-filled eyes.

It was true. In section B-2, Penny had lost it all.

She slowly collapsed to the sidewalk, the section of the paper gripped tightly to her chest. Men in suits rushed over to help, but she could not see a single face. Her eyes were being pecked away by images of stained forks and unwashed windows.

. . . . .

When Richmond burst into Jacob's room with the silver pistol, Jacob was lying in bed finishing his second novel of the evening. The moonlight shed a ghostly spotlight on his father, who stood towering above him like a Greek monument.

"I am not a coward," Richmond said quietly. "No matter what all of you think, I am not a coward."

Jacob pulled his sheets up to his nose, shaking in fear as a tiny wet pool soaked into his crotch. The gun glistened like a bright white chalk scraping through the darkness.

"I am not a coward," Richmond repeated. He spoke in a nervous but rhythmic cadence, like Hamlet at his soliloquy. "I was never a coward."

Jacob nodded.

"I'll prove to you that I'm not."

In one graceful movement, Richmond leaned against the wall and placed the tip of the gun into his mouth.

With a loud bang, the door slammed open and Valerie burst into the room, her hair disheveled like a mad clown's.

Standing before her was her husband, holding a gun in his mouth, facing her son, who was crying silently in bed.

"Oh God," she yelled out, throwing herself at Richmond.

The two, in a chaotic embrace, fell to the floor, the gun falling out of Richmond's grip.

"What are you doing here?" Richmond yelled, scrambling to get up.

"I thought you'd be married to him by now."

"I don't love Penny!" she screamed, a breath of alcohol filling the room. "I take it all back."

"What are you talking about?"

"I've been such a bad wife, a bad mother," she said, staring at her husband with manic eyes. "And I smell terrible!"

"You said you love him," Richmond said, grabbing her arm. "You were going to leave me."

"Richmond, I can't, I can't, I just can't," she pleaded. "I

can't be out there alone."

"We hate each other, Valerie," Richmond continued. "Go, go to Penny. Now."

"Let me stay," she pleaded.

"Go, or I'll shoot you first."

"Stop," Jacob said.

Richmond, still gripping his wife's arm, turned to his son. Across the room, Jacob stood with the gun pressed up coldly against his head.

"*I* am not the coward," he said.

Jacob pulled the trigger, releasing nothing but a hollow click and a faint fragrance of bravery that wafted through their home for the very first time.

Strawberry Fields Forever

Winter, 1999

The white lines disappear beneath my seat. I stare at these ephemeral points of focus, knowing they mean nothing. Mike steps on the gas and the lines start disappearing faster. I stop counting. 18.

Lost my lighter last night. The flint may have been dead anyway. The car lighter's broken too. Mike passes his smoke over. We have to keep passing the flame—it's a baton race straight to hell.

I take a prolonged drag, feeling the dry pain all the way down my throat. My lungs protest, but I keep the smoke in there for a while. I don't really exhale anymore. The smoke finds its own way out.

"What happens now?" I ask.

Mike is silent. I guess he doesn't hear.

"We wait until the funeral," he says.

I start counting the lines again. It's funny how fast they disappear. I wonder if the lines ever go the same way we do. It seems no matter what side of the road you're on, the lines go the opposite way.

We remain silent. I pick up an iced tea bottle from my feet.

"Whose is this?"

"I don't know. Not mine."

I put it back. I wonder about whose it is. The dirt all over it tells me that it's old. I flick my cigarette out the window as we approach a red light.

This pause in our drive is almost unbearably silent.

"You know," I say, to break the silence. "If life were a highway, it would have stop signs."

Mike doesn't turn to look at me. Maybe he can't hear. I don't really care anyway.

"And these stop signs······ they're there so you'll stop once in a while to take a breath. Maybe have a cigarette or two. And just reflect, you know, just think about all the distance you've crossed. Maybe, just maybe, these stop signs in our lives are good things."

In the corner of my eye, I see Mike nod. He's listening now, but I stop talking. I don't have much more to say. I turn the radio up, although neither of us is really listening.

It would have been the three of us—three pieces to a

three-piece puzzle—in this old station wagon. Damon and I would have surely fought for shotgun, simply so we could be the "DJ" and piss Mike off. The radio would never be left alone—stations would toggle erratically between hip-hop, rock, classical.

But silence is all we have now.

I glance over at Mike and see a tear on his cheek. I turn away and try to keep my sight out the passenger window, but my thought lingers on his tear. I wonder if I'm doing the same thing.

I recognize the music now. It's a Beatles' song. Lennon sings, "Let me take you down, 'cause I'm going to Strawberry Fields." I see that Mike's listening too.

Damon was a Beatles fanatic. Don't know if he liked this particular song. But I think it'll grow on me.

"You know what?" Mike says.

Not turning, I respond, "What?"

"When I stop at a stop sign, I don't think about the distance I've crossed," he says. "I just wish I never had to stop."

Pieces of You
ⓒ Tablo 2009

1판 1쇄 발행 2009년 2월 10일
1판 12쇄 발행 2023년 5월 30일

지은이 타블로

책임편집 변규미
편집 김지향 이희숙 박선주
일러스트 정은규(www.gaechaban.com)
디자인 윤종윤 이현정
제작 강신은 김동욱 임현식
마케팅 정민호 박치우 한민아 이민경 정경주 박진희 정유선 김수인
브랜딩 함유지 함근아 김희숙 고보미 박민재 정승민 배진성

펴낸이 이병률
펴낸곳 달
출판등록 2009년 5월 26일 제406-2009-000034호

주소 10881 경기도 파주시 회동길 455-3
✉ dal@munhak.com
🐦 f ⓘ dalpublishers
전화번호 031-8071-8683(편집부) 031-955-8890(마케팅)
팩스 031-8071-8672

ISBN 978-89-546-0757-5 03840